Judith Cook was born and b.... .....
She began her career as a journalist for the *Guardian* and
went on to become a freelance writer, winning awards
for investigative journalism and having several highly
acclaimed non-fiction books published, most notably *To
Brave Every Danger*, the epic story of highwaywoman
Mary Bryant. Judith Cook has also written two previous
novels, several plays and books about the theatre, and
she is a part-time lecturer in Elizabethan and Jacobean
theatre at Exeter University. She lives in the fishing port
of Newlyn, Cornwall, with her partner and two cats.

Praise for her novel about playwright Christopher
Marlowe, *The Slicing Edge of Death*:

'Judith Cook brings her investigative journalist skills
usefully to bear . . . along with a rattling good grip on the
plot. Cook's Marlowe is brilliant, witty, charismatic'
Guardian

'Cook roots her exciting and readable novel firmly in the
world of the playhouses'   *Financial Times*

'A good, pacy read . . . Cook is keen on fine historical
detail and has obviously mastered her subject'
Evening Standard

'A well-balanced thriller . . . intelligent and entertaining'
TLS

Also by Judith Cook

The Slicing Edge of Death
To Brave Every Danger

Death of a Lady's Maid

Judith Cook

HEADLINE

First published in 1997
by HEADLINE BOOK PUBLISHING

First published in paperback in 1998
by HEADLINE BOOK PUBLISHING

10 9 8 7 6 5 4 3

ISBN 0 7472 5608 X

Printed in England by
Clays Ltd, St Ives plc

HEADLINE BOOK PUBLISHING
A division of Hodder Headline PLC
338 Euston Road
London NW1 3BH

To Sylvia Parnell
for her constant encouragement.

ACKNOWLEDGEMENTS

My most heart-felt acknowledgement to Dr A. L. Rowse who edited and published extracts from the real Simon Forman's diary and casebook and presented him in such a sympathetic light. He long pushed me to write about Simon although I do not think this is what he had in mind!

Also to the present-day Royal College of Physicians for their assistance, and the Shakespeare Centre library in Stratford-on-Avon for the use of their invaluable facilities.

Chapter 1

Eliza 'after the Queen'

The body floated steadily down the river propelled swiftly now as the outgoing tide joined a current already swollen with the unseasonable rain. It slowed however as it bobbed against one of the piers of London Bridge, an obstacle which impeded its progress enough for it to begin drifting over towards the rapidly falling water of the south bank, where it lay just beneath the surface, temporarily buoyed up by its skirts. It was there the wherryman found it.

He had risen in the dark hour before dawn as he did every day of his working life and, after downing a stale quart of ale and chewing on a crust, made his way through the driving rain to the watersteps upriver from Westminster where he kept his boat. In any normal year the weather towards the end of June would have been good and there would have been a crowd of customers waiting for him but 1591 was not a normal year. A harsh winter had been followed by the coldest and wettest spring in living memory and there were ominous signs that the Plague might again be stalking the streets.

The wherryman plied his trade wherever it was likely

to be most profitable, and his practice in early summer was to start the day upstream to ferry the early lavender pickers to the Wandsworth Fields, but now the lavender was rotting before it had chance to bloom. However, out of habit he took up his usual station, and finally a lone figure appeared out of the darkness, a young lad wrapped in an old cloak. He stepped shivering into the boat and mumbled for the wherryman to take him down to the other side of London Bridge as he was late for work.

So the wherryman bent to his oars, taking advantage of the outgoing tide. Lights were beginning to appear dimly along both banks as the damp rain clung to their faces and there was a brackish smell from the Thames. The swift flow of the current brought them quickly down towards the bridge and the wherryman was preparing to shoot his boat expertly under its arches when an oar hit something just below the surface of the water.

'What's up?' enquired his passenger.

The wherryman grunted. 'Dunno. Something in the water. Here, hold this oar and try and keep us steady while I take a look.' He knelt down and, still holding his own oar in a firm grip, leant over the side and attempted to free it from the soggy mass which had wrapped round it. Whatever was keeping the oar where it was suddenly released its hold, and as the oar freed, the wherryman realised he was dealing with a body. It wasn't all that uncommon; careless drunks, victims of street assaults and ruined young women all too often ended up in the river. His heard sank. City regulations and the licensing rules ordered that any wherryman finding a body in the river was to bring it ashore and inform the relevant authorities straight away; finding those authorities could be a long and tedious process. A dull streak heralded a dismal dawn but at least with the light the wherryman might find some business. However, if he did the right thing and beached the body, found a constable and made an official report, it could take half the day and he'd lose valuable earning time. 'Hell's teeth!' he swore.

'What is it?' asked his passenger with increasing irritation as he struggled with the heavy oar.

'A poxy floater. That's the morning gone, unless . . .' The boatman paused and then added, 'Don't just sit there gawping, help me get it into the boat. It was no easy task for although they were out of the main run of the tide, the current was still flowing swiftly seawards. It took them several attempts before they managed to haul the dripping burden over the side and into the boat, by which time they were both drenched and the wherry had shipped a good deal of water. They looked down at the catch. The body was that of a young girl. Sightless eyes stared up at them out of a waxen face.

As the boat drifted out midstream once more the wherryman looked back upriver to where a light shone from a house close to the water's edge. He made up his mind. Settling again to his oars he began to pull away in the direction of the light.

'Here, where are we going?' asked his startled fare. 'I told you I was late for work and now you're taking me back the way we've come.'

'How was I to know I'd find a floater?' responded the

wherryman. 'But since I've not got all day to hang around and see to it, I'm going to take it to Dr Forman. He'll know what to do.'

The lad's jaw dropped. 'The necromancer?'

'Dr Forman's no necromancer. He lanced an abscess on my neck something wonderful last year. People'll say anything.' The wherryman guided the boat back into the main current and made for the light.

At about the same time the body surfaced a man emerged on to the street from a small house in a Bankside alleyway, well wrapped against the weather and carrying a large leather bag. He sighed as the door closed behind him for there was nothing he could do. As he set off back home, his mind dwelt on the woman he had just left. It was Simon Forman's custom to rise early to write up the notes of his previous day's consultations for his Casebook, but on this particular morning he'd been knocked up at three o'clock by the husband of the old woman who kept the fruit and vegetable stall by the Green Dragon. He'd opened the door to him himself.

'It's Sara,' the old man had said, near to tears. 'She's mortal bad. Will you come? Here's a florin, it's all we have.'

Simon waved it away. 'Go back to her, tell her I'll dress and come directly. Is it the cough again?'

The old man nodded. 'It tears her apart. But now she has a fever and breathes like this.' He made a panting sound. 'And she's wandering in her mind. Asked me to go for a priest! I said, all right, I'd fetch the parson but she said no, the priest. She's forgot now we don't have priests.'

After dressing, Simon went to his study, poured poppy syrup and an infusion of white horehound into two small phials, put them with two other items into his bag, then made his way to his patient. Her husband took him upstairs to where she tossed and turned on the straw mattress of the marital bed. The room, poorly furnished but clean, was lit only by a rush dipped in a saucer of oil. Simon took two candles out of his bag and lit them for he always carried some with him when visiting poor houses; good candles were costly and many households economised on light.

Gently he bent over the woman. There was little need to examine her for he could see at once she was near to death, suffering from that affliction of the lungs that carried off so many old people when they took sick and the weather was cold or damp. He turned to the old man. 'This is now in God's hands, though at least I can ease her. You need a woman's help. Go to Rose Alley and see if Mother Baker's there and tell her Dr Forman asks if she'll come here.' The old man hesitated. 'I'll pay her fee. Your wife's kept me in excellent fruit and vegetables ever since I came back to London.'

Simon turned to the woman, lifted her head, and spooned some of the horehound into her mouth. After a brief interval she stopped turning on her pillow and opened her eyes, looking fretfully for her husband. Then she focused on Simon. 'It's good of you to come, Doctor,' she whispered, 'but we both know it's no good. I'm going to die, aren't I?' He nodded for he would not lie to her. 'Then go home and get the rest of your sleep. The money in the stocking under the mattress will be more use paying for my funeral than for you.'

She patted his hand and he took it. 'Your money's safe where it is. This is in payment for all the apples and oranges you've given me over the last two years.'

She smiled, then a look of distress crossed her face and she struggled to sit up. 'I fear, I fear . . .'

'So do we all, Sara, whether or not we know the time of it,' responded Simon.

'No, Doctor, it's not dying I'm afraid of, it's what comes after. I was born in the days of the Old Religion when you confessed your sins to the priest and if you repented them, then he asked God to forgive you. But now there are no such priests.' She began to cry. 'And I'm dying having committed a mortal sin. Will *you* hear my confession?'

'Heaven help me, Sara, I'm no man of God! Far from it. You won't make me believe you've committed a sin so dire you need fear God Almighty on Judgement Day,' Simon replied but she would not be comforted and so he heard her out. Her husband had been a sailor when they married and it was a good marriage, but childless, a sad state she'd had to accept as God's will. But when she was nearly forty, and her man away at sea, a pedlar had come to the door, a man with a merry brown face, rings in his ears and a roving eye.

'God forgive me, I'd never strayed before, even in thought, and he must have been ten years younger than me, but he'd a way with him and it was spring, May month.' For two weeks they'd been lovers, then off he'd gone and she'd never seen him again. Within weeks she knew she was with child. 'It seemed like a miracle. But I couldn't face my good man with another's child when he came home.'

'And the baby?' asked Simon.

'She was born in the February, a winter child, and an easy birth even though I was forty. I was delivered secretly at my sister's house in the country and she brought the child up as one of her own. I've not seen my daughter now for many years and she's never known I was her mother.' She struggled for breath. 'Now she'll never know.'

'If that's your terrible sin, Sara, then most of mankind is guilty of it – and me more than most,' Simon added ruefully, knowing how prone he was to that particular temptation. 'I'm no priest, but I truly believe you've nothing to fear. God must have enough accounts to settle with the corrupt and evil without concerning himself over a woman who bore a child out of love. If all who have been so tempted were cast out, then Heaven must be an empty place and Purgatory a full one! Now, I'll give you some poppy syrup to make you sleep.' He settled her down as her husband returned, accompanied by a comfortable-looking woman. Simon drew her one side and put a coin in her hand. 'If she wakes again, give her some more of the syrup. It'll not be long.'

Simon had been so deep in thought that he had reached the watersteps next to his house before realising it. He glanced down and saw a wherry putting in. It seemed to be labouring and low in the water. The wherry-

7

man jumped out and, passing the rope through the large ring on the wall, called up, 'Here, give us a hand, will you? We've picked up a floater.'

Simon sighed, visions of a hearty breakfast receding as he put down his bag and took off his cloak. He went carefully down the slippery steps. 'Well,' said the wherryman, 'if this isn't a bit of luck. I was on my way to find you, Dr Forman.' His passenger, looking with some apprehension at the alleged necromancer, saw only a man of middle height in his mid thirties. He wasn't strictly handsome, but good looking enough with lively brown eyes and a skin darkened by sun, suggesting he had spent some time in foreign parts. Droplets of water clung to his dark reddish hair and a gold earring glinted in one ear. He didn't look like one who had dealings with the Devil.

Together the three men heaved the body out of the boat and on to the bottom steps. It was very heavy with water. 'Wait here,' said Simon, 'I'll fetch my servant to give us a hand to get her up to the top.'

He returned almost at once with a large, grizzled man whose face was puckered by an old sword cut; he was grumbling loudly. John Bradedge, never at his best in the early morning, couldn't see why the poxy wherryman couldn't have dealt with the matter himself, a point he made clear to the wherryman who retorted that he had sought Dr Forman for advice because he had once consulted him over the matter of an abscess on his neck, and he had seemed a good man to turn to.

They carried the body to the top of the steps and laid it down on the quay. Long fair hair spread out like a wet veil, to which the gloomy light of dawn gave a greenish tinge. It reminded Simon of the fine weed that grew on ponds and along the edges of the sluggish rivers in May month in the Wiltshire countryside where he was born. The weed had blossomed with small white flowers which gave off an unpleasant smell. The body, however, did not, which suggested the girl was newly dead. He bent down and turned her face towards him, then peered closer. 'God's death!' he exclaimed. 'I know her!'

After they had got the dead girl into an outbuilding at the back of his house, Simon sent the wherryman and his passenger about their business and went into the house with his servant. He was met by John's wife, Anna, a child of about eighteen months balanced on her hip. She was familiar enough with Simon now to scold him for the state he was in, telling him she would see to his breakfast while he changed out of his wet clothes.

Half an hour later, having breakfasted, Simon returned to the outbuilding. Although it was now daylight, it was still dark and gloomy and he had left a candle flickering in its holder. The only sound was a stead drip of water from the clothes and hair of the dead girl. He opened the shutters to let in what light there was, picked up the candle and looked closely at the body, remembering how the girl had consulted him some four months earlier. She'd arrived at his house without an appointment, demanding to have her horoscope cast. The first thing he'd noticed was that her colouring was unusual, the hair showing under her cap so fair it was almost white, as were her eyebrows, while her eyes were a very pale blue. She was slender, though full-bosomed, the kind of figure he often found tempting although not on this occasion. Susceptible as he was, there was something about this girl, an aura of frigidity, which almost repelled him. She reminded him of a small cat. Her pale grey dress was neat and of good quality but without ornament; he had put her down as a lady's maid.

He had explained to her that he could not produce her horoscope while she waited. 'I'll have to write down the answers to all the questions I must ask you, including the date of your birth and the time of day at which you were born. But I'm a busy man with patients to see, and a good horoscope takes time to cast. Come back in two days and I'll have it ready for you. I take it you can read?' he added.

She nodded. But when it came to personal details, she gave him little in the way of information. She was called, she said, Eliza, 'after the Queen', and her father was head groom on a country estate, her mother in charge of the dairy, but she would not say where. Her age was seventeen years and she had been born on the tenth of July 1573: 'My mother said I was born just as the sun came up.' But throughout the girl seemed to be giving Simon only half her attention. Her glance strayed around the room he used both as a study and for consultations. The walls were lined with shelves carrying an array of jars and bottles of all sizes and shapes, boxes of small phials, pestles and mortars, unpleasant-looking metal instruments and a number of leather-bound books. After more prodding Eliza had then, reluctantly, given him a few more details concerning her health, constitution and appetite.

While he sat making careful notes, she began to prowl softly round the room examining the charts and maps of the heavens pinned on one wall, stopping before the large five-pointed star painted on the floor. It seemed to fascinate her. She stopped and turned to him. 'Is it true you can raise the Devil, Dr Forman?'

Simon sighed. 'God's death, girl, I'm not Dr Faustus! You've spent too long in the playhouses.' He had then got up to show her out, adding, 'But it would help if only you were more open with me. You're very young. What is it you hope your horoscope will show you?'

She'd regarded him steadily with those strange pale eyes. 'That I shall have wealth.' That surprised him. It was usually young men who demanded such information. Was she hoping to be left money? A dowry, perhaps?

'You have expectations?'

'You could say that,' she replied without a smile.

'And that's all? You don't want to know if you'll soon have a lover or a husband, and who it's likely to be? That's what most young women want to know.'

'But I'm not like most young women,' she said. He was opening the door to show her out, when suddenly she stopped and turned to him. 'Tell me one thing, Dr Forman. Is it true a maid cannot conceive the first time she goes with a man?'

In spite of himself he laughed. 'Is that what this is all about? If that's what your young man's told you, Eliza, then it's to be hoped he's ready to call the banns and buy the ring! It's quite possible to conceive on such an

11

occasion. Are you promised in marriage after all then?' Amused at what appeared to be the first sign of feminine doubt, he patted her on the shoulder.

She flinched away and stiffened. 'I've no young man and no plans to marry.'

'Then be warned,' he told her. 'Whoever's spun you this yarn, has probably done so to other ignorant girls.'

She said nothing in response to this except to arrange when to return for her horoscope. As Simon watched her go, he pondered her last question. If not a suitor, then who? The son of the house? A young gallant who had asked a substantial price for a fresh young virgin? He marvelled at how, in spite of centuries of experience, young women still fell for the same old story: the procession of weeping girls who had presented themselves to him for advice over the years testified to that.

Eliza duly returned two days later. He had found her horoscope difficult to cast, in part because she had been so reticent but also because there seemed to be a shadow he could not explain over her future. She listened, unsmiling, as he went through the chart with her: wealth, yes, but after that . . . He simply couldn't see clearly. Therefore, he told her, there would be no charge, suggesting she return in a few weeks' time so that he could try again. She took the short chart from him, thanked him, then said, 'My mistress asks, since you're a physician, if you'll give me a strong sleeping draught for her. She's been without sleep now for many nights and needs her rest.'

'Then it's best she comes here herself or sends for me to visit her,' Simon replied.

Once again she'd given him one of her strange looks. 'I'll tell her that, but in the meantime will you let me have such a draught? She suffers greatly.'

Reluctantly, he'd poured a dose into a tiny phial for her, saying, 'Here, take this. It's a weak syrup of poppies. She must take it before retiring either as it is or in wine.'

She'd looked far from pleased. 'Is that all you'll give me?'

'It's all I'll give you or anyone without seeing them myself. Poppy syrup, strong or weak, must be treated with respect. That will ensure a sound night's sleep but if the problem is deep-seated, I must know the cause and treat it with something milder. Juice of lettuce boiled with roses is effective and far safer. Tell that to your mistress.'

She looked as if she were about to argue but then shrugged, paid him for it and went on her way. He had never seen Eliza again, nor so far as he was aware, had he been consulted by anyone who might be her mistress. And now she was dead. He had been right to see a shadow over her life. Whatever misgivings he might have had about her when she was alive, in death he could feel nothing but pity for the girl who had been called Eliza, 'after the Queen'. Simon sighed and went in search of his man.

John Bradedge was in the scullery assiduously cleaning his master's riding boots, grumbling loudly to his wife who was scrubbing the big deal table in the large kitchen while their child sat on the floor on a blanket chewing a crust. In spite of the dark morning, the kitchen was bright from the light of the fire as was everything in it. Anna was very houseproud.

But however much John might grumble, and he was a chronic grumbler, he recognised his good fortune in having met up with Dr Forman. His youth, as his mother never ceased to tell all and sundry, had been misspent. Born in Cheapside, then apprenticed to a silversmith, he'd been an idle lad, interested only in drink, girls and card-playing. Turned out by his exasperated master (and pursued by a young woman who claimed her bastard child was his), he'd rapidly left London for the Low Countries where he'd joined the army. It was there he had met Anna and married her, only when the wars ended to find himself discharged back home with no money, nowhere to live and a child expected within days. Simon had found them sitting side by side outside St Saviour's churchyard with nothing to eat but too frightened to beg. After learning of their plight, he had taken them back to his own house, given them an attic room and, within the week, had delivered the child himself, which was as well, as the boy had come into the world the wrong way up.

A few days later Simon spoke to them both at length explaining that he had only recently moved back to London from abroad and was looking for a good man-servant and a housekeeper. If they were agreeable to his terms, then he would be prepared to take them on in that capacity for a trial period of a month. If they were satisfactory then they could stay on and he'd give them good quarters and fair wages in exchange for which he demanded hard work, loyalty and their solemn promise that they would say nothing outside the house of what they saw and heard. A doctor must keep many matters private.

That was well over a year ago and so far it was working out to everyone's satisfaction, though the doctor's ways had taken some getting used to. His house must be kept clean and neat at all times, which was no hardship for Anna who had grown up in Leyden, although the standard he demanded would be considered extreme in most English households. As to his own person, he regularly took a bath every week, sometimes twice a week: the Queen's own majesty was considered wildly eccentric for bathing regularly every three weeks. And rain or shine the doctor rose each day at six o'clock even when he'd entertained a woman overnight, would haul up a bucket from the well, plunge his head into it, then breakfast before retiring to write up his everlasting notes. The discipline only varied when he was called out to a patient.

John's grumbles stopped in mid flow as Simon appeared at his usual brisk trot. 'Put the boots down, fetch a bowl of water and a cloth and follow me,' he ordered. 'And bring some more candles. It's still as dark as Hades out there. Oh, and send one of the lads with that medicine I made up for old Master Horner. I need you outside.' John did as he was told, then followed his master outside. Simon held the candle to the girl's face and then asked, 'Don't you also recognise her?'

John looked again, scratched his head, then remembered. 'She looks different with her hair dark from the water, but didn't she come for a horoscope, let me think now, around the beginning of February?'

'She did indeed. Now let's see what we can find out before we tell the authorities.'

John looked doubtful. 'Is that wise, sir? There's bound to be a Crowner's 'quest.'

'Undoubtedly. But there's no harm in seeing what we can learn first. Help me unlace her. Now then, you've worked with me now long enough, tell me how long you think she's been dead, bearing in mind she was found in the river.' They turned the body over and unlaced her bodice from the back, carefully peeling it off the now stiffening arms. Then they unlaced and removed the skirt.

John felt the arms and legs and then the trunk. 'The death stiffening is happening and as the corpse's been in the water this might mean—'

'That it will have cooled sooner than one might expect. That's right. Indeed I believe she died no later than late last night or even the early hours of this morning.'

Under her gown the girl wore a fine cotton petticoat and shift, both edged with narrow lace. Simon examined her carefully. Apart from the marks on the face, already noted, there appeared to be no other injuries.

John looked at her dispassionately. 'Reckon we know how she died, don't we? She drowned.'

'Possibly.' Simon delicately raised an eyelid for earlier he had closed her eyes for decency's sake. He thought how strange her pupils looked. Almost black. Yet he remembered her as having the strangest of pale eyes. 'She talked of coming into wealth, of having unspecified expectations. So why should she end up in the Thames?'

'Perhaps she was with child and her lover jilted her, so she drowned herself. It's a common enough tale.'

'Let's see.' Simon raised the girl's shift above her waist. The abdomen was slightly swollen. 'You could be right.' Gently he palpated the swelling. 'Yes. I'd say she would be, oh some three months' forward, maybe even a little more.'

'Well, that's that then, isn't it, sir? She couldn't face her mistress or dare tell her family. If you tell the Crowner so, there's an end of it.' John couldn't understand why anyone should go to such trouble over one more dead girl.

'Maybe,' replied Simon, thinking again of old Sara and her bastard child. He regarded the body again. 'I must ask the authorities to remove her so the coroner can sit and I'll also send to him to say that I'm willing to attend the Inquest. As for suicide . . . I don't know, but I'd like to raise doubts otherwise they'll bury her at a crossroads instead of in the churchyard. Now think back, are you sure she never said anything to you on either of her visits that might be worth recalling?'

A dreadful thought struck John and he was beginning to voice it when he looked at his master's face and decided not to do so, so cleared his throat instead and shook his head. Simon looked keenly at his servant, sensing his unease. Did he know something he preferred not to divulge? He decided to leave it for the present.

Together and with difficulty due to the rapidly stiffening limbs, they began dressing her again. It was while pulling on the skirt that John felt something small and round, like a coin, under the waist of the petticoat.

He investigated and found a tiny pocket, inside which was not a coin but a pendant and a valuable one at that, made of gold with a circle of small rubies surrounding a coat of arms. It hung from a golden chain. He handed it to Simon. 'A rich ornament for a servant, don't you think, sir?'

Simon held it up to the light. 'Very. It must be worth a tidy sum.'

'There you are then, Doctor, she stole it and ran away.' John sounded triumphant. 'She was frightened of being caught and hanged.'

Simon ran his finger over the pendant. 'Why should she do that? If she left London and sold it somewhere many miles away, she'd have money enough to keep her and her child for years. I don't recognise the arms as belonging to one of the great houses, but then every wealthy merchant with money to spare can buy himself a title these days.'

His man peered over his shoulder. 'I think, sir, though I'd not swear to it, that I've seen this coat of arms on the gate of a big house off Bishopsgate.'

'Then get over there and see. If it turns out to be the case, find out from the local tradesmen or the landlady in the nearest tavern whose household it is and the kind of state they keep. You know what to do by now. As for me, the morning's half over. When I've informed the Constable and sent word to the coroner I must get on with the work of the day.'

They eased the girl's bodice back into place and it was while inserting her arm into the long sleeve that Simon saw something he had previously missed. 'Look there, John. See? A faint mark round this wrist.' Quickly he picked up the other arm. 'And here, too. The same. At some time her wrists were bound, not tightly enough to cut the flesh, but certainly enough to mark it. This is no suicide. She was tied up before she went into the river.'

Chapter 2
Olivia

The rain had stopped but the day was still dark and overcast as John Bradedge set off across London Bridge for Bishopsgate. Lights flared in the booths on each side of the thoroughfare, which was surprisingly empty for a morning in June. As a rule he would have had to fight his way through people pushing in opposite directions: shoppers haggling over cloth or wine, purposeful artisans on their way from the Bankside to the City, out-of-town tourists fresh from gawping at the rotting heads decorating the entrance on the north side. It was one of the great sights of London, a bridge which was a whole street of shops and houses. Now weeks of bad weather coupled with fear of Plague kept the crowds away.

But if the bridge had been thronged with dancing girls from the Ottoman harems undulating to the music of the sirens, John would hardly have noticed, he was so lost in his own concerns. Of course he should have confessed everything to his master straight away but as things were going so well, and the doctor trusting him to assist with more and more aspects of his work, why should he risk jeopardising the best employment he'd ever had or was likely to have? But then came the question of trust.

But it wasn't as if he'd deliberately broken the rules, was it? Hadn't he acted in all good faith? It was true he hadn't recognised Eliza until he'd looked a second time, but when the doctor not only asked if he remembered her, but also if she'd said anything to him which could be to the point, surely then should have been the time to own up. What if it turned out he held vital information?

For the truth was that a week after Eliza had gone off with her unfinished horoscope and sleeping draught, she'd returned once again. John had told her Dr Forman was out and unlikely to be back for some time but she said she already knew that as she'd just encountered him outside St Paul's and explained she'd been on her way to buy more poppy syrup for her mistress. The doctor had informed her he'd a number of patients to see but had told her to go to his house and ask John Bradedge to put some poppy syrup into a large phial for her. Now one of the things Simon had spelled out to John right from the start was never to give anything at all to a patient, however harmless. 'You may well feel tempted if I'm not here, but they must be told to wait. What's wrong may seem obvious but you have no skill in recognising symptoms and you could send them away with a harmful draught or ointment due to a wrong diagnosis. When you've worked with me a few years then I'll be happy to let you loose with ointments for sores or liniments for rheumatic joints, but not yet. Promise me you'll do what I say?' Of course John had promised.

Yet it had seemed all right. The girl was adamant that Forman himself had told her she could collect the medicine. So he'd gone with her into the doctor's study, selected a bottle of poppy syrup from the back of a row of such bottles and given it to her, but when she offered to pay him he was at a loss. He had had no idea what to charge. In the end she'd given him half a sovereign and he'd put it in the box, already half full, in which Simon kept payments from patients. Simon believed in charging those who could afford it a substantial sum as this enabled him to ask little or nothing of those who could not. Whilst John realised he'd broken the house rule it wasn't until after Eliza had gone that he began to feel really uneasy about it and he had honestly meant to tell the doctor what he had done as soon as he returned, hoping, in fact, that Simon would ask him if he'd given the poppy syrup to the girl. But Simon had said nothing at all and a whole evening had passed without anything being said, and after that he'd kept putting it off. Eventually as no harm seemed to have been done and Simon hadn't discovered that half a bottle of his mixture was missing he'd almost forgotten about it. But surely there couldn't be a connection?

John's thoughts had carried him not only over the bridge but into Bishopsgate with its warehouses, churches and merchants' houses, most of the latter securely gated and largely hidden from the road. It did not take him long to find what he was looking for, a pair of newish iron gates, in the middle of each of which was set a painted wooden shield bearing a coat of arms. Surreptitiously, he took the pendant out of his pocket and checked. It was definitely the same. Now all he had to do was find out who lived there.

He was just debating whether to start his enquiries at a nearby baker's shop or try the tavern on the corner when the gates opened and two men, tradesmen from their appearance, emerged into the street after an acrimonious exchange with a gloomy-looking porter who carefully relocked the gates behind them. As they passed him John turned and looked fixedly at a poster, illegally pasted up on the wall, advertising the fact that the Lord Admiral's Men would be presenting Master Marlowe's play of *Tamburlaine the Great* that afternoon at two o'clock at the Rose Theatre. Out of the corner of his eye, John saw the men cross the road and enter the Blue Boar Tavern and immediately followed them inside.

The morning was now well advanced and the tavern was quiet, most people being about their work. The tradesmen were sitting at a table in the almost empty taproom and were calling to a boy to bring them some ale.

John tapped the lad on the shoulder. 'And a quart for me, too, boy.' He then sat himself firmly down on the bench opposite the two men, adding, 'Mind if I join you?' They both shrugged, one noting that it was a public house and folk were free to sit where they chose. John waited until his tankard arrived, took an almighty swig, then asked casually if his companions knew who owned the large house on the corner.

'Sir Wolford Barnes,' one replied, 'the merchant venturer. Why do you want to know?'

'Because I'm looking for good employment. Finding work isn't all that easy for those of us back from the wars in the Low Countries.' John fingered his scar as he spoke.

'You don't look particularly hard up,' said the second man, critically scanning John's good quality stuff doublet and breeches.

'Had a bit of luck over in Holland,' invented John, hastily. 'Made a few crowns on the side, but they're fast running out. What I need is for someone to put me in the way of finding work as a manservant here in the City.'

The first man spat on the floor thoughtfully. 'Don't know how much there's going over the road. What d'you think, Harry? You've got a girl working there.'

'Couldn't really say,' replied his mate, 'seeing as we don't work there. Will and me just supply the kitchen with vegetables, cheese and eggs. We've been coming now every week for, oh, close on seven years. I'll say one thing for Sir Wolford, though: he pays on the nail, not like some.'

'Certainly not like that good-for-nothing son-in-law he's got himself,' broke in Will. 'They say he runs up debts everywhere and Sir Wolford's always having to pay them off for him. Harry's girl's under-cook over there and she knows a thing or two about what goes on, I can tell you. There was some panic on today, wasn't there, Harry?'

Harry nodded. 'Her ladyship's maid's gone missing and she's raging. Says she can't manage without the girl. My girl couldn't stand her, said she gave herself airs and graces like she was the mistress of the house.'

John heaved a silent sigh of relief. This was going to be easy. Perhaps he could find out enough for the doctor to forgive him about Eliza. 'You two gents like some more ale?' he asked. 'It's on me.'

* * *

John returned to Lambeth just after two, only slightly the worse for wear after the morning's steady drinking. Simon was aware that his servant could drink most men under the table and had a head like teak. Simon's morning had been a busy one. Half a dozen people had come with minor complaints such as coughs and colds brought on by the bad weather, and for them he had prescribed draughts of horehound or angelica. Then there was a large sweaty fellow with boils that needed the lance followed by an application of ointment made from the plant known as cuckoo-pint, then a carpenter who had hit his thumb instead of a nail. Next had been an alderman wanting his horoscope cast to see whether or not his young wife was faithful to him (on average there were about two of these a week), and a young mercer's wife to see if she was with child again. The latter consultation had been slightly embarrassing for them both. When Anna told him young Mistress Walsh was waiting to see him, he'd looked up her previous treatment in his Casebook. At the bottom of the careful notes he'd made was a small star next to the word 'haleked'. This was his secret code for noting those ladies who had wanted to pay him without using money and whose offers he'd taken up. He'd told old Sara nothing more than the truth. He was susceptible and he'd found himself solicited on a number of occasions by all kinds of women, from young whores to mature merchants' wives.

After she'd left, not without casting moon eyes over his face and letting her hand linger in his, he'd eaten his dinner then turned again to the Casebook and looked up the dead girl. Yes, there she was. 'Eliza— ?' he had written. A brief paragraph noted the results of the horoscope and the fact that he had dispensed a small phial of poppy syrup for her unknown mistress. He was still staring at the notes when John put his head round the door and asked if he could come in.

'Of course, man. So what have you to tell me?'

John, his stomach still rumbling from large quantities of ale, began at the beginning with his seeing the coat of arms in Bishopsgate and discovering it belonged to Sir Wolford Barnes, a merchant venturer in good standing both in the City and at Court. 'He's thought of as a hard but fair master and he has a large household. Got his knighthood a couple of years ago for services to the Crown: the usual thing, a big gift to the Queen, payouts to influential officials . . .'

Their tongues loosened with drink, Harry and Will had become increasingly talkative. Several months earlier Sir Wolford had married his daughter off to a young waster called Sir Marcus Tuckett, heir to a title and big estates in Kent. 'His father's a lord and it seems it's a straight business deal. Sir Wolford wanted his daughter to end up Lady something or other; Tuckett's father needed the money. By all accounts young Tuckett is a waster and there's been problems finding him a bride,' John told Simon.

'And what about the lady?'

'I'm coming to that. Seemingly she's a tasty piece with a hot eye, a very hot eye. There's been plenty of gossip. First she played around with an actor so openly her father had to forbid her going near the playhouses altogether. Next it seems there was something going on between her and her father's secretary. So all in all the sooner she was married off before there was a real scandal, the better. Tuckett's father's ailing and the only thing he cares about before he dies is that there's a grandchild to ensure the succession.'

'You seem remarkably well informed. And is the lady obliging her lord in that direction?'

'Not yet. One of the tradesmen I spoke to has a girl there who's an under-cook and listens to what goes on – you know how it is in these big houses. She told him Tuckett complains his wife'll hardly let him near her to make it a possibility and doesn't care who knows it. Their quarrels are public knowledge. Tuckett says he's fed up, as before his marriage he was bedding anything in a skirt that'd have him and even some who didn't!'

Simon smiled thoughtfully. 'You've done well, John, very well. Not without cost, I imagine?'

'I did rather have to ply the lads with ale, sir. And then there was the game pie.'

Simon took out his purse and handed John a crown. 'That should cover everything with something over for the trouble you've taken.'

John thanked him, then gave him the real news. 'There's one more thing. Apparently there's been a big to-do at Sir Wolford's today. My lady's personal maid hasn't been seen since yesterday morning.'

Simon stood up and rubbed his hands. 'I've a goldsmith to see on Cheapside this afternoon. I think afterwards I should pay a visit to Sir Wolford to see if anyone recognises the pendant.'

It was well into the afternoon when he finally arrived at Sir Wolford's gate and briskly pulled the rope attached to the bell hanging in the archway over it. Simon had to pull it again before the glum-looking porter appeared, gave him a dismissive look and demanded to know his business. 'Dr Simon Forman to see your master.'

'He 'asn't sent for no doctor,' responded the porter. 'If he 'ad they'd-a told me.'

'I've not been called in for a medical consultation, my good man. I've a matter of urgent and confidential business to discuss with him. Will you go and tell him that? And also that it might be better if he hears what I have to tell him before he learns of it from the Coroner of Lambeth's clerk!' The porter shuffled away, leaving him outside the gate cooling his heels for a good five minutes during which time whenever a cart passed by he had to dodge the evil-smelling spray from the kennel that ran down the middle of the street. When the porter returned, he opened the gate and let Simon in, nodding in the direction of the house, a fine timbered one, which was tucked out of sight behind the high wall. After such a reception, Simon was preparing himself to be told to use the tradesmen's entrance but in the event he was shown in through the front door and told to wait in the hall.

He looked around, trying to get a feel of the place. The hall was panelled in oak and hung around with pictures. Facing him was an enormous portrait of a stout gentleman dressed in a plum-coloured doublet, much embellished with copper lace. His hand was lightly placed on a globe, while in the background a fleet of ships could be seen. This had to be the merchant venturer himself. On one side of it was a smaller painting of a thin-faced, rather dismal middle-aged woman, wearing an unflattering bright pink gown; she, presumably, was the lady of the house. On the other side was a larger portrait of a simpering blonde, her hair elaborately dressed, wearing an even more elaborate gown of pale blue silk embroidered with flowers. A huge ruff of the finest lace surrounded her neck which was also hung around with several necklaces, one of pearls. Sir Wolford obviously believed in putting all his goods in the shop window. The young woman was much as Simon imagined she'd be, pretty in a doll-like way and not very bright. She and her husband were probably well matched.

There was a cough from behind him. A dark young man, elegantly dressed in dark grey was claiming his attention. 'Dr Forman? I'm Francis Down, Sir Wolford's secretary. Would you come this way, please? Sir Wolford and Lady Tuckett will see you now.' From his air of authority, Simon deduced he considered himself to be a very superior employee indeed.

Down led Simon through a long passageway past open doors through which he could see several grand rooms furnished in great style. But the chamber that he was finally shown into was obviously very much a living room. It smelled strongly of dog and several large hounds were sleeping on the far from fresh rushes strewn on the floor, while the walls were hung with faded, slightly moth-eaten tapestries. Dr Forman had obviously not been considered of sufficient importance to merit being received in one of the better chambers.

Sir Wolford, more soberly dressed but easily recognisable from his portrait, was seated at a table busily signing papers. The young woman staring out of the window with her back to the room must be his daughter, Lady Tuckett, judging from her intricate coils of golden hair. Unlike her father she was showily dressed in a dark red gown trimmed with gold, stretched over a large hooped farthingale.

Simon bowed and introduced himself. Sir Wolford looked up impatiently. 'Well then, Doctor – er – Forman, tell us what this is all about, and be quick as I've no time to waste. I've an appointment in the City before the end of the afternoon.'

'I'll get straight to the point then,' replied Simon, briskly. 'The body of a young woman was brought to me this morning. A waterman had found her in the Thames.'

'And what's that got to do with me?' Sir Wolford queried.

Simon produced the pendant and handed it to the merchant. 'Because of this.'

Sir Wolford stared at it intently then called to his daughter who had continued to stare out of the window, showing no interest in the proceedings. 'God's death, Olivia! Look at this! Surely it's the very pendant I gave you on your wedding day.'

At this the woman turned round and Simon received a

severe jolt. The simpering portrait of the vapid young woman in the hall had done no justice either to her or to her father who presumably had paid for it. Olivia Tuckett was truly beautiful, with a fine-boned face and perfect features, but it was her eyes that unnerved him, not only because of their colour, brown being a rarity with such fair hair, but because of the intelligence that shone out of them. She appeared to have everything: remarkable looks and a bright mind. No wonder her family and her husband had their hands full. She came over to her father, took the pendant from him, then turned to Simon. 'Where did you find this?'

'On the dead woman. It was in her pocket. It fell to me to examine the body before it was taken away for the Inquest. I was trying to identify her and this was the only item she had on her. I recognised the coat of arms,' he lied smoothly, 'having noticed it on your gate. Then my manservant who was on business for me hereabouts earlier in the day told me that a search was being made for a missing servant from your household.'

'I see.' She looked at the pendant again. 'My maid's been missing since yesterday morning. Are you saying it's her?' She did not seem in any way surprised.

Simon regarded her thoughtfully. 'It seems very likely. Perhaps you could send someone down to identify the body. It lies in the stable behind the Anchor on the Bankside until tomorrow's Inquest. The coroner is already posting notices to see if anyone knows who she is.'

The lady said nothing but returned Simon's look. Sir

Wolford, uneasily aware that there was an undercurrent he did not understand, rose firmly to his feet. 'Well, thank you for your trouble, Doctor,' he said, obviously intending to bring the interview to an end. 'I'll send my secretary, Francis Down, along to the Anchor to see if he recognises your young woman. Now I must be off. If you've anything more to tell, you'd best talk to my daughter. It's her affair. Oh, and what do I owe you for your trouble?' Obviously Sir Wolford was used to paying for commodities brought into his household and saw Simon as just another trades-man who had arrived with something to sell.

'I'm a doctor of medicine, Sir Wolford,' he told the merchant sharply, 'and am paid only in that capacity. On this occasion I'm merely acting as a good citizen.'

Olivia Tuckett waited until the door had closed behind her father then turned again to Simon. The glance she then cast over him was appreciative, indeed, encouraging. He decided her reputation was probably well earned. 'Well?' she said. 'I presume there's more?'

Briefly Simon explained how Eliza had consulted him the previous February to have her horoscope cast and that when she'd returned for it, she'd asked for a sleeping draught for her mistress. 'I gave her poppy syrup, suf-ficient for a single dose, and told her that if more was needed I must see her mistress in person. Have you any recollection of this?'

'Possibly,' she replied, still looking him in the eyes. She moved closer to him in a drift of expensive perfume, then said abruptly, 'This dead girl, what does she look like?'

'About your height and of similar build. Flaxen hair,

almost white. Eyes which, when she was alive, were very pale blue.'

Olivia Tuckett considered this. 'Yes, that could well be Eliza.'

'Then it must be the same girl,' responded Simon, 'for that's the name she gave to me when she came to see me, Eliza "after the Queen". But she refused to tell me her family name even when I asked for it to cast her horoscope. She said only that her parents were servants on a country estate.'

'That is our estate in the Dedham Vale. Both her parents are servants of ours; indeed her mother is most highly regarded by my own. My mother spends most of her time in the country,' she explained, 'her health is not good. Well, no doubt we'll find out for certain when Francis returns.' She looked again at the pendant. 'I missed this some weeks ago but did not want to upset my father by telling him. I thought perhaps—' She broke off, then continued, 'It never crossed my mind Eliza might have stolen it. She's been my maid since she was fourteen and a very good one too, most discreet and always honest. How sad! The temptation must have been too much for her and then, when she realised what she'd done, the poor girl drowned herself rather than confess to me.' The words sounded fine, even sympathetic, but to Simon they did not ring true.

'Maybe,' said Simon, 'it's a plausible explanation, except that I'm almost sure she didn't take her own life. I believe she may have already been dead before she went into the river some time last night.'

Olivia considered this and seemed on the point of replying when the door burst open and a young man entered the room. He was dressed in the height of fashion, his doublet slashed and tucked, his sleeves sewn with loveknots. But his clothes were stained, his face flushed and bloated, and he smelled of a mixture of stale wine and sweat. He was not a handsome man, his eyes were too small and he had a weak chin. This, thought Simon, had to be the Tuckett heir. What a match for such a woman!

Tuckett focused his eyes on the pair of them with some difficulty, staggered slightly, then hicupped. 'Who's this then, Livvy? Your fancy man?'

Olivia made no attempt to conceal her disgust. 'This, Marcus, is Dr Forman. He came to inform us that a poor girl found in the river this morning might well be Eliza.'

'Dr Forman?' Tuckett swept a wavering eye over Simon. 'Not *the* Dr Forman – well, well, well. Haven't you heard of him, Livvy? A man of many parts, it's said. Doses your pox, casts your horoscope, and throws a little alchemy in for good measure. That's right, isn't it, Doctor?'

Simon nodded. 'I'll take my leave, Lady Tuckett. If you want my help at any time, then my house is down river, not far from the church of St Saviour. Anyone will direct you.' He turned to go but Tuckett blocked his way. 'So that sly little bitch ended up in the river, did she? Never took to her.' He leered at Simon. 'Now you've told Livvy where you practise I'll send her along. I'm sure the good doctor knows all about love potions, Livvy. Give her a good dose for me, will you Doctor? She's cold as charity.'

It was then Simon dropped his stone into the pool to see what ripples it might make. 'Oh,' he said, 'there was one other thing, Lady Tuckett. Your maid was some three months' forward with child. Did you know?'

'I did not.' The lady's face, as was fashionable, was painted, but under the cosmetics she went visibly white. Faint beads of sweat gathered on her forehead.

Tuckett guffawed. 'Well now, there's a quaint conceit! That whey-faced slut with child! It's more than you've been able to manage, isn't it Livvy?' Simon went out, leaving them staring at each other.

Chapter 3

Crowner's 'Quest

As a rule sleep came easily to Simon, especially when he had previously suffered a broken night, but the events of this day proved too intrusive, circling round and round in his head in an endless diorama: the dripping body being hauled out of the water, the discovery of who the girl was and his conjectures of what might have happened to her, Sir Wolford Barnes's household with all its many tensions and his meeting with the beautiful Olivia. The faces of the two young women, one white and lifeless, the other brimming with vitality, swam before him.

The memory of the dead girl's hair floating like waterweed in a Wiltshire pond brought back much he preferred to forget. An absent father who may or may not have married his indifferent mother, an education which had begun at the free school across the meadow from home and had continued, unusually for a boy in his circumstances, at the grammar school in Salisbury where his teachers had prophesied a brilliant career. But there had been neither money nor interest to encourage his going on, as he'd ardently desired, to Oxford. Like the rest of his class he could look forward only to a life of labouring or, at best, that of an honest artisan.

Yet he had yearned for the opportunity to study the new learning that was setting fire to the imaginations of his supposed betters, the study of the stars, mathematics and, most of all, medicine. Then, to compound matters, he had fallen foul of a local landowner who had already taken a hearty dislike to a lad he felt had ideas well above his station. Arguments over the enclosure of common land had led to violence on both sides, while protestations that he had been wrongly picked out as a ringleader fell on deaf ears; with the result that he spent the next twelve months in the local gaol.

Emerging with the label of a troublemaker with no future, Simon did what so many young footloose men had before him and set off for Europe as a soldier of fortune, picking up medical knowledge as he went along, often on the battlefield. He found to his great satisfaction that he had a decided aptitude for it. Finally, with money saved and having picked up Italian on his travels, he had gone to Italy and enrolled as a student of medicine and astrology at the University of Milan where he did well and might have prospered and stayed in Italy for the rest of his life except that he was homesick for England. Sometimes he felt he had made the wrong decision. Coming home had reminded him, in spite of his qualifications and skills, of the gulf that yawned between him and the well-educated sons of the wealthy who proudly called themselves physicians.

It was the early hours of the morning before Simon's overactive brain quietened down and he finally fell into an uneasy slumber from which he woke unrefreshed. He had also overslept. By the time he left his bed and ran downstairs, yawning, to the water pump it was well after nine o'clock and the Inquest was due to start sharp on half-past nine. Back in his room he dressed carefully for the event in sober black, over which he put his long gown to denote his professional standing. He felt extremely annoyed with himself: now there would be no chance to write up his notes from the previous day's patients. Waving aside Anna's offer of breakfast, he downed a pint of ale and, chewing on an apple, went into his consulting room to put out two phials of medicine and a jar of ointment, and then shouted for John Bradedge.

He appeared carrying his master's well-polished boots and his rapier in its hanger. Simon sat down, pulling on his boots. 'I've left a note where these are to be taken,' he said motioning towards the medicines. 'You can take them round now.'

'What about this?' John flourished the sword as Simon made for the front door. He hesitated for a moment, then shook his head. Wearing a sword was difficult with the long academic gown and anyway as a physician he did not always go armed even though many respectable citizens never ventured outside their doors without feeling the comfort of their swords at their sides.

Simon emerged from the house into a watery sunshine. The day was an improvement on the last but it was still unusually cold with a cutting east wind stirring the surface of the Thames into choppy waves. Out on the water he could see a number of boatmen looking like water beetles as they struggled to ferry their passengers across the river.

He closed the door behind him and turned to find old Sara's husband crossing the street towards him. Aware now that he had barely time enough to reach the Anchor he simply hadn't the heart to ignore the old man for it was clear from his face what had happened. 'She's gone to God then?' Simon asked.

The old man's eyes brimmed with tears. 'As the tide turned, at about four o'clock. As easy as a child. The draught you gave her quietened her and she went in her sleep holding on to my hand. She was a good woman, a good wife to me. Forty years we'd been together and in all that time she never gave me a moment's sorrow, never played me false. It was cruel the Lord made her barren and there are no sons or daughters to see her to her grave.' He scrubbed away the tears. 'She's to be buried tomorrow. Is it possible you could come, sir?'

'If I can I will.' Simon patted the old man's arm. 'It was for the best. The disease was eating her lungs and she was fighting for every breath. But now I must get on or I'll be late for a Crowner's 'quest.'

He debated briefly whether to take the road beside the river where he might well be held up by all the commercial activity going on along the waterfront or risk cutting through the maze of lanes and alleyways which made up the domain of the Bishop of Winchester on the Bankside. In the event he chose the latter and set off at a brisk pace. As he did so a fellow who had been lounging against the wall of the house opposite straightened himself up and set off a few paces behind.

Once into the Bankside proper, Simon cursed himself

for obviously having made the wrong choice. The slight improvement in the weather had brought out crowds of people, all of whom seemed to be going in the opposite direction to himself, forcing him either to push his way through them or risk getting his feet covered in mud or worse from the kennels running down the middle of the wider lanes. He was unaware of the man following him, his face now half-concealed by a scarf.

As the clock of St Saviour's rang the half hour Simon knew he would not arrive in time. The way ahead was not only full of people but was also blocked by two carts which had met head on, their drivers roaring at each other to give way. On his right was a narrow dark passageway between two warehouses close to the Bear Pit which, he seemed to remember, should lead him back to the water-front again within a stone's throw of the Anchor. It looked most uninviting. It was very dark and he could hear the sound of water dripping from its roof and running down the walls; there was a strong smell of urine; obviously it was put to use by the public as a latrine. With a feeling of unease Simon hesitated for a moment outside, looking behind him. He seemed to be alone and there was no logical reason not to take the short cut with his pressing need for haste. Without more ado, he plunged into the darkness, his boots sounding a muffled echo.

He was about halfway down the alleyway when he became aware that something was wrong. Sensing rather than hearing anything, he whipped round to find a man, his face half-concealed, coming up behind him, his up-raised hand holding a dagger obviously intended for his back. Simon's reaction was fast and immediate. He tried to grab his assailant's wrist but he was hampered by his gown, the narrowness of the passageway and the ground beneath which was slippery with water. For several minutes the two men grappled with each other in silence, apart for the sound of the laboured breathing, until Simon finally succeeded in gripping the man's wrist so strongly that he was forced to drop the weapon; but not before Simon felt its point graze along the side of his hand. Foiled in his attempt, the man turned and fled back the way he had come.

Simon looked after him, sucking the cut. There was no time to pursue the man and even if there had been, he doubted there'd be any point. By the time he'd retraced his steps, his would-be killer would have vanished into the hidden warrens of the Bankside. He shrugged, then quickly made his way out of the passage and into the daylight to examine what damage had been inflicted. The cut on his hand was not serious but it was sufficiently deep to drip blood. Swearing to himself, Simon wound his kerchief around the wound, knotting it with his teeth, and trusted it would suffice until after he had given his evidence and returned home. He was now within sight of the Anchor and very late. The Inquest would have started without him. But in spite of this, Simon did not continue at once towards the inn but remained for a few minutes where he was, staring unseeingly at the busy river. If his assailant had been an ordinary cutpurse, surely he would merely have knocked him to the ground and stolen his purse, not tried to kill him.

* * *

The public benches in the large room on the first floor of the Anchor Inn were barely half full. There were the usual ghouls who got a thrill out of looking at the dead body and hearing the gory details of its demise, and a few, mainly elderly, householders with nothing better to do in the way of entertainment, one of whom, old George, was a fixture at all Southwark Inquests and even some further afield. Several middle-aged women, obviously neighbours, had taken their places in a corner and brought their knitting with them. Had the corpse been either that of a notorious villain or a man or woman of substance, the benches would have been packed but as word had got round that the dead woman was merely a servant there was only moderate interest. The room was chilly and smelled of stale drink and infrequently washed woollen clothing.

Precisely at nine-thirty the door opened and a Constable appeared solemnly preceding a small elderly man in a lawyer's gown who was holding a pomander to his face. Behind him came the Clerk of Court carrying rolls of parchment, an inkpot and several quill pens. These he put down on a table in front of the chair to be used by the coroner.

'Corpse can't be anyone that matters,' muttered George to his neighbour, 'otherwise it'd be Coroner Danby, not bad-tempered old Monkton.'

'You will all rise,' announced the clerk, who then read from a scroll: 'This Inquisition is held today to inquire into the death of one Elizabeth Pargeter, the proceedings being before Her Majesty's Coroner, Sir Thomas Monkton. This Inquisition is called at Southwark, in the county of Kent, on the twentieth day of June 1591 in the thirty-fourth year of the reign of Elizabeth, by the Grace of God, Queen of England, France and Ireland, Queen Defender of the Faith, in the presence of the said Sir Thomas Monkton upon the view of the body of Elizabeth Pargeter there lying dead. The jury will now take the oath.'

There was the noise of tramping feet as the sixteen members of the jury entered the room after having viewed Eliza's body in the inn's stable. Each one in turn swore the oath on the Bible placed before them by the clerk, giving their names and occupations. They were obviously respectable citizens of the merchant or superior artisan class and mostly of middle-age.

'You have viewed the body?' enquired Monkton.

'We have, your honour,' they chorused.

'Have you elected one among you to act as Foreman?'

'We have decided it shall be Christopher Mountjoy, Master Wigmaker and Hatter,' said one of the men.

'Thank you, you may all be seated.' Monkton looked at the bench where the witnesses usually sat, the only occupant of which was a young dark man neatly dressed in grey.

The coroner frowned. 'I thought Dr Forman was to attend and give evidence.'

'So he is, sir,' the clerk replied. 'It would seem he has been delayed.'

'Well the proceedings can hardly be held up to await his pleasure,' said Monkton sourly, causing the young man on the witnesses' bench to smile to himself, 'so shall we proceed?'

The clerk stood up and cleared his throat. 'We are here today to examine the cause of death of Elizabeth Pargeter, the body of this woman having been found in the River Thames on the morning of the nineteenth of June in this year of Grace 1591, by one Will Hudson, waterman.'

'Is the waterman present?' asked Monkton.

'No, sir. Dr Forman was to speak for him so that he was free to ply his trade.'

'All the more reason for his being here and on time,' muttered Monkton. 'Is there a witness who can positively identify the body?' The clerk motioned to the young man sitting on the bench who immediately stood up. Monkton turned towards him. 'Your name and occupation, sir?'

'Francis Down, Sir Thomas. Personal secretary to Sir Wolford Barnes, merchant venturer of the City of London.'

'Be pleased to take oath, Master Down,' said the clerk. As Down moved to do so the door at the back opened and Simon appeared. The coroner motioned for the proceedings to stop while Down looked at the new arrival as if assessing the situation. 'You are late, Dr Forman,' barked Monkton. 'Perhaps you might care to inform us why you have shown such discourtesy to this Inquisition?'

Simon held up his right hand which was swathed in the now blood-soaked kerchief. 'My humble apologies but I was delayed. Unfortunately I was attacked by a cutpurse on my way here and sustained this injury.' There was an immediate buzz of noise from the public benches as people turned to tell each other how things were now so bad that a man couldn't walk in safety along the public highway in broad daylight, let alone at night, above which the voice of old George could be heard informing everyone that in his day young people 'was made to behave like Christians – they should be taken as little children to Tyburn to see the hangings like I was when I was but a little tacker and told that's what they'll come to if they break the law'. His neighbour was beginning loudly to agree with him when the clerk called for order.

'We will proceed then,' said Monkton. 'You may sit down, Dr Forman. It is certainly a sign of the times in which we live that you have been set on in such a manner. Continue, Master Down, if you will.'

Without giving Simon another glance, Down turned to the coroner. 'I can swear that the body of the young woman in the coffin outside is that of Elizabeth Pargeter, personal maid to Lady Olivia Tuckett, wife to Sir Marcus Tuckett and daughter of Sir Wolford Barnes.'

'Have you any idea why she might have been discovered in such case?'

'No, sir. The Lady Olivia first discovered she was missing two days ago and questioned the other servants as to her whereabouts but none knew. My lady was surprised at her absence as she was a good and reliable servant.'

The coroner considered this. 'It is of course possible that she fell into the river by accident but in matters of this nature one question must always be asked. Do you know of any reason why she might have taken her own life?'

'No, sir. But,' he added, 'she was always of a secretive nature and it might be that there are others who do.'

'There is no question of her having been turned out by her mistress for some misdemeanour?'

'That I can certainly answer. There was no question of it. As I've already said, sir, she was considered a good servant and so was much in my lady's confidence.'

'Has she any family?'

'Her parents are servants on Sir Wolford's country estate. As soon as I had viewed the body last evening and confirmed it was that of Eliza, my lady sent at once to tell them what had happened.'

'Thank you, you may sit down. Now, Dr Forman?'

Simon took the oath and stood before the coroner giving his place of residence as the Bankside and his occupation as physician and surgeon.

'Your qualifications?' asked the coroner. 'It is unusual to find a man of your standing in a court of this nature. You are, I presume, properly recognised?'

Simon sighed. 'I trained in Milan, sir. But I am recognised here by the University of Cambridge and also by the Royal College of Physicians.' By the latter body most grudgingly, he thought but did not say.

Monkton leaned forward. 'Tell us, if you will, how you came to be involved in this affair.'

'I was on my way home from seeing a patient and was passing the top of the watersteps near my house, when I looked down and saw a boatman and his passenger trying to heave what appeared to be the body of a woman out of the boat and up the steps. They called to me to help them, which I did. It was immediately obvious that the girl was dead and when I saw her I recognised her as one who had come to me for advice some four months back. As the waterman was already losing business, I suggested she be carried to my house until the authorities could be informed.'

'I see.' Monkton frowned. 'And what advice did she want from you?'

'She wanted her horoscope cast to see if she would have good fortune,' replied Simon, bending the truth, 'as many young girls do. And also to ask for a sleeping draught for her mistress.'

'Did she say who her mistress was?'

'No, sir, she did not. I gave her a small phial of weak poppy juice which is much prescribed in such circumstances, but warned her that if her mistress wanted any more, then she must come in person for it is not a medicine to be taken lightly. As to her horoscope, I found it hard to cast, presumably because she had no future, poor girl.'

Monkton looked down at a note he had in front of him. 'I understand you examined the body? Why was that?'

'Because as a doctor, I thought it might be helpful to this court.'

Monkton looked unconvinced. 'Surely there is no dispute? The girl drowned. All there is to decide is whether this was by mischance or intent.'

'She did indeed drown, sir. But I have to say here and now that I do not consider it was either by accident or because she wished to end her life.' His statement provoked another buzz of noise in the room, leading to the clerk informing those on the public benches that if it happened again he would clear the court.

Simon continued, 'On looking at the body closely, I saw her wrists had recently been tied tightly with thin rope – the marks can still be clearly seen if you care to take a look, and from the change in the size and colour of the pupils of her eyes when I saw her first, I would say she had been given some drug, possibly an opiate like poppy juice, perhaps to prevent a struggle.'

'You are saying then that she was put into the river with malice aforethought?' queried Monkton in no little amazement.

'I can see no other explanation. It might also interest you to know that my examination also showed that she was some three months' forward with child.'

Monkton banged the table in front of him in exasperation. 'But surely there you have given us the best of all reasons why she might do away with herself? Her fear of bringing shame on her family and on the household of Sir Wolford Barnes.'

'That might well be the case, sir, but she would hardly have drugged herself then asked someone to tie her up before doing so.'

The coroner looked far from pleased. 'I had been going to ask both of you gentlemen if you thought it possible the girl had fallen into the river by accident, but it would seem that Dr Forman at least has already made up his mind. What do you say, Master Down?'

Francis stood up again. 'I cannot say, sir. Since we do not know where she went into the water it's hard to judge whether or not she fell in by chance; there are, of course, many hazardous places beside the river. But it still doesn't explain why she chose to leave our household. However, if it is true, as Dr Forman says, that Eliza was with child then, as you said yourself sir, it would appear to provide a possible explanation as to why she might take her own life.'

'And Dr Forman's notion that she was constrained in some way before her death, the inference being that she was put into the river by some unknown person or persons?'

'I'm no doctor,' Francis Down replied modestly, 'but it sounds somewhat unlikely. I have no way of knowing whether it could be true or not. But if you want my opinion then it is that Eliza must, sadly, have taken her own life.'

The coroner considered this and then said, 'Thank you, gentlemen. You may both sit down. You, Dr Forman, will no doubt wish to return home as soon as possible to see to that wound.' Blood was now seeping steadily through the makeshift bandage. Then turning to the jury, Monkton continued, 'Gentlemen, you have heard from Master Down that he personally knows of no reason why this girl might have taken her own life, although he does not rule out the possibility, and from Dr Forman that she was with child and that he believed she had been constrained in some manner before her death. That, of course, is merely his opinion. The third possibility is that the girl slipped or fell into the river purely by mischance but, as Master Down has said, it is difficult to decide whether such an accident could have occurred without our knowing also where it took place. It is, therefore, for you to decide whether her death was accidental, whether she took her own life by drowning – and remember we have learned that she was to bear a bastard child – or, as Dr Forman has said, that she was constrained in some way, leading to the suggestion that she was forcibly put into the water, which would be wilful murder.'

The jury filed out and Monkton held a whispered conversation with the clerk while Simon and Francis Down sat side by side on the bench in uneasy silence.

Francis Down broke it first. 'You've made much drama of this, Dr Forman. Isn't it possible you could be wrong? Surely the marks, if indeed there are such, could be from some other cause? She might have scratched her arms on undergrowth or trees somewhere on the bank upriver or have been bruised by flotsam in the water. I'd been inclined to think it an accident until you told us of the child. Suicide is now the most likely explanation.'

Simon, who had not taken to Down when they'd met the previous day, found his initial reaction hardening into positive dislike. 'I've made no mistake. The marks of the cord can clearly be seen on both wrists. Go look for yourself. She was probably alive but helpless when she was put in the river to drown.'

Down eyed the bloodstained kerchief. 'A nasty cut. You were lucky, perhaps, that it wasn't worse.'

'Indeed I was,' said Simon, 'since I have the strangest feeling that my attacker was no ordinary cutpurse. Possibly I should put it about that I began learning my skill as a physician during the wars in the Low Countries. In fair fight with a rapier I think I can match with most. Please feel free to circulate this information where it might prove useful.'

But before Down could reply, the jury filed back into the room and the clerk called on all present to stand. 'You have reached a verdict?' Monkton asked Mountjoy.

'With difficulty, sir. It was clear to us that the girl did have a reason for taking her life, but if Dr Forman, who is expert in such matters, considers that she was constrained by bonds before her death then it would suggest that this was done by evil purpose and with intent. Neither verdict would be a happy one but in the circumstances we have decided finally to take the latter view: that Elizabeth Pargeter met her death at the hands of a person or persons unknown.'

'I see.' Monkton was clearly annoyed for the verdict meant that further enquiries would now have to be made. 'And this is the opinion of you all?'

'It is, sir.'

Monkton cleared his throat. 'Very well then. Since it has been decided that she did not take her own life, she can therefore be afforded Christian burial. Those who wish to claim her body must now see to its removal. Otherwise it will be put in a pauper's grave.'

Francis Down stood up. 'My mistress has given me money to have her body decently coffined and taken to her parents in Essex for burial.'

'Then see to it!' barked Monkton and swept out.

Chapter 4

Advice from a Secretary

Anna was in the kitchen ladling stew into a bowl for her husband when Simon arrived back from the Inquest. Both exclaimed with concern when they saw his bandaged and bloody hand. 'Put some warm water out for me, will you Anna? And find some strips of linen while I look for a salve to put on it,' he called to them as he walked through to his study. He reappeared a few minutes later with a small bottle. Gingerly he unwrapped his stained kerchief and examined the cut. It was long, running from below the third finger to the side of the hand just above the wrist, but it was no longer bleeding profusely, and after washing it and dabbing it with the salve he asked Anna to bind it tightly for him. He then joined them at table.

'So what happened?' asked John as Simon attacked hungrily a plate of beef and turnips.

'I was set on by some fellow in the passageway under Henslowe's warehouse by the Bear Pit.'

His servant snorted. 'There must be two villains for every honest man on the Bankside.'

Simon agreed but decided to share his own misgivings. 'Maybe, but I don't think this was your usual petty thief. He crept up behind me, made no attempt to cut my purse,

and seemed ready to have stabbed me in the back. Nor,'
he continued as John was about to break in again, 'would
there have been room to fight the man with a sword even
if I'd had mine with me. The passageway's far too narrow
to draw a weapon, something my man must have considered. No, I think I was singled out for a specific reason,
though why that should be and what the reason, I'm not
at all sure.'

John forbore to reply. He found his master's fascination
for looking into the doubtful affairs of others hard to
fathom when surely he had more than enough to do
doctoring.

Simon thought back to the result of the Inquest.
Obviously the coroner had been greatly irritated by his
evidence and annoyed at its influence on the verdict. No
doubt Sir Thomas Monkton knew of Sir Wolford Barnes
and his wealth, may even have known him personally, and
anyway was unable to understand why so much fuss
should be made over the death of a mere servant girl. But
for Simon's own intervention, any suspicions regarding
the manner of that death would have been swept under
the carpet while the law, the City and the gentry, in the
person of the callow Sir Marcus Tuckett, closed ranks to
ensure there would be no public scandal. Simon smiled
ruefully at his own reaction yet again to the attitude of the
powerful to those beneath them. When Sir Giles Estcourt
of Quidhampton had condemned him to gaol at the age
of sixteen, he had been given a lesson on how the strong
regarded the weak that would remain with him for the
rest of his life.

Now he found it impossible to put Eliza's death out of his mind. Susceptible as he was to women, Simon could truly say that it was not any attraction she might have had for him that made him want to know the reason for her death but a matter of simple justice. Then there was the business of the attack made on him that morning. Maybe it was merely a coincidence and had nothing whatsoever to do with his visit to Sir Wolford Barnes's household the previous day and yet . . . He thought back to the reactions of the lovely Olivia Tuckett and her husband. Would either of them be capable of arranging for someone to see to it that he never got to the Inquest? And what of Eliza's family? What must they be making of it all? Whatever they might feel, as both her father and mother were employed by Sir Wolford and his wife on their Essex estate, they were hardly in a position to demand the truth be uncovered when their roof and their livelihoods depended on Sir Wolford Barnes.

It was now Wednesday. If Eliza's body was taken from the Anchor straight after the Inquest, it would still be well into the following day before it reached its destination and even if her parents were now aware of the tragedy, as Down had told the coroner, her funeral would need to be arranged and her grave dug. Therefore it was likely to be Friday before her burial could take place. Simon went into his study and consulted his diary to see if there was anything urgently requiring his attention over the next few days. There was little that was pressing. He made up his mind. Might the clue to the girl's death lie not in London but back in Essex? Perhaps it had nothing whatsoever to do with the merchant venturer's household, but, more mundanely, was rooted in the jealousy of some lovesick swain left behind in the country. He determined he would do his best to find out.

Thinking of Eliza's funeral reminded him of that of old Sara, due to take place the following morning. He would go to it as promised and then ride to Stratford St Anne in the Dedham Vale, taking John Bradedge with him. To this end he told his servant to see to it that his horse was brought from where it was stabled and made ready for him by mid morning and that John should also hire one for himself.

Simon was not the only one with much on his mind. Francis Down also had a great deal to occupy him as the room cleared after the Inquest. First he went down to the stable and looked again at Eliza's body. He chewed his lip as he looked at the girl's arms now decorously crossed on her breast and saw for himself the marks Dr Forman had claimed were made by ropes. Her eyes were now closed and he did not feel inclined to lift the lids to examine the pupils. He stood looking at her thoughtfully for some time before he turned away.

After arranging to buy a suitable coffin off a nearby carpenter, he then went in search of a reliable carrier. He told him the nature of the burden he wanted taken into Essex and paid him to leave London with it for his master's estate outside Stratford St Anne just as soon as the girl had been put in the coffin and its lid securely closed on her. It was essential, Francis told him, that he reach the girl's home as early as possible the next day. He then went into the nearest Ordinary and ordered the dish of the day.

He ate his pie surrounded by noisy diners whose table manners left a great deal to be desired. Usually this would have irritated him, but now he scarcely noticed as he recalled the events of the morning and the doubts surrounding Eliza's death. In some ways they had been two of a kind, he and Eliza. Both from similar backgrounds, both ambitious and determined to better themselves. Francis was also the child of servants on a large estate, but in his case the old lord, a widower, had taken a fancy to the only son of his wife's maid and had encouraged him to learn to read and write. When Francis's father died suddenly of a fever, the old man had stepped in and paid for the boy to go to the nearby grammar school to further his education, telling his mother that he had plans for him when he was older. If Francis did well he might even help him to university with a view to his taking Holy Orders. But as luck would have it his benefactor died, to be succeeded by a son who had always disliked Francis and been jealous of the attention his father had paid to the boy.

Francis had left at once for London and immediately set about finding a foothold on the ladder to better things. He had worked for a number of masters, gradually gaining a reputation for his secretarial skills, coupled with discretion and a shrewd wit. He allowed nothing to stand in his way: even his mother's illness and subsequent death did not draw him away from the city. He had come to the attention of Sir Wolford some five years earlier when his then employer, an acquaintance of the merchant's, had learned that he was in need of a good secretary who was both reliable and discreet. As he was cutting down on his own household he recommended the young man to Sir Wolford, and thus Francis Down had joined the Barnes's household.

After leaving the Ordinary he returned again to the carrier to make sure his orders were understood, and was relieved to find the coffin had already been collected from the Anchor and that the man was about to set out. He then walked back through the Bankside to London Bridge, crossed it, and so arrived back at Sir Wolford's house early in the afternoon. It was very quiet as his master was away doing business in the City.

Olivia Tuckett was on her way to her private chamber when he confronted her. As she attempted to pass him Francis put his arm across the narrow passageway barring her path. 'Why such haste, lady?' he enquired. 'Surely you want to know what happened?'

She tried unsuccessfully to push him away. 'I want to hear as little as possible. Eliza's dead and will soon be buried. She can't be brought back. It's over.'

He caught her by the shoulder. 'If that's what you believe then there are most certainly things you need to know. First that Dr Simon Forman is alive and well, and was thus able to give his evidence to the coroner. I presume it was on your orders that some clumsy dolt tried to prevent his doing so?' He could see by her face that he was right. 'I credited you with more wit. Very well, while

Forman's intervention in this affair couldn't have been foreseen, it was a most foolish move. There are better ways of dealing with him, should it be necessary, when the time is ripe. All you have succeeded in doing is confirming him in his belief that the girl met her death by foul play. Oh no, this affair is most certainly *not* over, Olivia, it's not over at all. At the end of the day the verdict was wilful murder.'

'Murder!' She paled. 'What are you saying? It can't be.'

'Now do you see why we need to talk? And this is hardly the place for it.'

She glanced uneasily over her shoulder then reluctantly ushered him into her room. 'Very well. But be quick and say what you have to say. It's most hazardous to risk either Father or Marcus finding us here together.'

'You have not always been so careful,' said Down, closing the door behind them and leaning against it. She turned away from him impatiently as he continued. 'The best your fellow could do was slash the good doctor's hand when the two grappled with each other, after which he fled. The attack only delayed Forman's arrival at the Inquest by a matter of minutes – but now with his mind made up. Had some less dramatic means have been found to detain him, an urgent call to a supposed sick patient or death bed, then the jury would have been asked to decide only whether the girl slipped or threw herself in the river, whether or not it had emerged that she was with child. But murder would never have come into it.

'As it is,' Down went on relentlessly, 'Forman not only told the Inquest of the child, which if he'd left it there would most probably have resulted in a suitable verdict, but went on to tell of rope marks, a strange look to the eyes and his belief there'd been foul play.' He moved towards her. 'Be advised. Leave Forman alone – for the time being. What's needed now is a time of quiet so the matter can be forgotten. The death of a lady's maid by foul means or otherwise is of no importance and the verdict obviously annoyed the coroner. To this end too I suggest you write to him explaining that you were too upset to do so previously but that now, on hearing the verdict, you feel he should know that the girl had a violent lover against whom you'd warned her many times and also that a piece of jewellery had vanished with her which was returned to your father by Dr Forman.'

Olivia shook her head. 'I've already told you. I'll have no more to do with it.'

Down moved over to her and gripped her tightly by the arms. 'Oh no, lady, it's too late for that. By casting me in the role you have, you've also placed yourself at my side.'

She tried to break free 'Why are you doing this? Do you too now want money?'

He laughed. 'You know very well what I want.'

She looked at him in desperation. 'Very well, I was foolish to persuade an incompetent servant to set on Dr Forman. But surely he must be silenced now before he does any more damage? I don't think he will let it rest. Can't you see to it for me?'

Francis Down continued gripping her arms but said nothing.

'Here,' she cried, pulling a ring from her finger, 'this

belonged to my grandmother, the stone's a ruby. It must be worth five hundred guineas.'

'You offer me a ring for the life of a man? And the first death not yet accounted for? Lady, you still owe your reckoning. As to Forman, he's no unsuspecting girl without background, and he's now forewarned, so much so that he took pains to warn me that he could be a dangerous antagonist. I believe him. I tell you again, leave him alone for the time being.' He pulled her to him and kissed her roughly. 'I don't want your ring, Olivia. At the very least I want things to be between us as they once were. A single hour in your bed during your husband's absence isn't nearly enough. We're two halves of a coin, you and I. You should have married me.'

She struggled against him. 'Are you mad? Think of the distance in station God has put between us.' She tried again to break loose, freed one of her arms and hit him hard across the face. He winced, and then dragged her over to the long mirror hanging on the wall, pushing her face close to it beside his own. 'Look into your conscience, lady, and read me there. It's a true book. You'll find me there your equal.' He let her go and looked round the room.

'You've pen and paper. Write now to the coroner.' He left her staring into the glass, tears of rage running down her face.

Chapter 5

Country Matters

The weather the next morning had very definitely improved, with glimpses of sun and a stiff breeze which brought the tidal smell of the open sea into the stale alleyways of the Bankside. As Simon set off for Sara's funeral he breathed in the welcome fresh air and was grateful that it looked as though he was unlikely to get soaked during his long ride that day.

A small group of mourners had already gathered in the churchyard to say their last farewells. Among them were regular customers who had bought their fruit from the old woman, a handful of her neighbours and, standing next to Sara's husband, a plump middle-aged woman in a respectable brown cloak and kirtle accompanied by a younger woman in dark velvet. Sara's husband shook Simon warmly by the hand then turned to introduce him to the two women. 'This is Sara's sister, Mary, and my niece.'

Simon greeted the two women and asked Sara's sister if she had come far.

'From Kent. I came at once as soon as I had the message that our Sara was so sick,' she said sadly, 'but it seems she was gone before I'd even reached my daughter's house in the City. My daughter had been out of London with her husband and didn't know of her aunt's sickness until it was too late.' She patted the younger woman on the arm. 'She is my youngest child, Avisa.'

Simon looked at the girl with interest. This then must be Sara's lovechild. She was an attractive young woman with a creamy skin and large, very dark eyes, presumably inherited from her gypsy father. She had a fine-boned face and her hair, from what he could see of it from under the neat married-woman's lace-trimmed cap, was also dark. 'So you live in the City?' he said.

'Since my marriage,' she replied in a quiet voice.

'My daughter's wed to William Allen, the silk merchant,' Mary informed him with some pride, then turned to speak to her brother-in-law.

Simon gave Avisa a further appraising look which she returned, a faint flush creeping into her cheeks. But before he could say anything more to her a down-at-heel curate arrived to take the brief burial service. There was no money to spare for the trimmings of bell, hymns and extra prayers.

The coffin was then lowered into the grave, the mourners threw on to it their handfuls of soil and sprigs of herbs or flowers, and then dispersed, a few, Mary and Avisa among them, preparing to return to Sara's small house with her husband. Simon again expressed his condolences.

Avisa Allen really was a most attractive young woman, thought Simon as he returned briskly to his house. Presumably she had no idea that she had just witnessed the burial of her true mother.

* * *

By mid morning Simon and John were crossing London Bridge on horseback. The tide was low and along the foreshore at Blackfriars they could see women, their skirts kilted to their knees, picking the wild radishes that grew on the bank above the tideline. The two men made their way eastwards through the narrow streets of the City, past the warehouses and mansions of the merchants safe behind their high gates, and so out into the Aldgate and into a different world. The lure of the fast-growing capital sucked in the rural poor who were convinced there were fortunes to be made. Within a ten-minute ride of the merchants' houses inside the City walls, clusters of poor dwellings had sprung up, outside which feral, barefoot children, with the faces of old men and women, played among piles of refuse.

One or two lobbed stones at the two riders as they passed by, causing John to drop back and threaten them with the short cudgel he always took with him on such journeys.

'Sewer rats!' he shouted as a rock narrowly missed him. 'Born to be hanged every one of you!' He urged his horse forward until he caught up with his master. 'No doubt their older brothers are already expert cutpurses while their sisters whore.'

Simon agreed. 'No doubt you're right, but what chance have they if they've no trade to offer and they have no employment? What worries me even more is the fear of their spreading disease. There have already been both Plague and fever deaths. If either take root here, they will spread and we will have another epidemic.'

Once outside the sprawling suburbs they moved at a brisk trot, their road at one point taking them across the bleak Wanstead flats, notorious for highway robbers and footpads. John again took a firm hold of his cudgel but all was quiet and they reached the Gallows Cross without incident before turning north-east where the road ran through a string of small hamlets. The welcome sunshine showed up only too clearly the water-logged fields and blighted orchards. It would be a poor harvest.

Simon's haste to press on meant that they stopped on the outskirts of Chelmsford only to change horses and for a quick quart of ale to wash down the bread and cheese Anna had given them. The sight of steaming plates being carried into the taproom did little to improve John's temper, leading him to mutter that at the very least they might have had a proper dinner before continuing on what he considered a wild goose chase.

'Stop grumbling, man,' Simon told him, draining the last of his ale. 'The faster we get on, the sooner you can sit in front of a piece of beef or mutton. If the girl's to be buried tomorrow, we've no time to waste.'

The further east they rode, the worse the road became. A long hard frost followed by weeks of rain had pitted it with deep potholes, reducing it in places to little more than a broad rutted track. They rode through the busy centre of Colchester in the gathering dusk and it was after eight o'clock before Simon drew rein before a handsome half-timbered inn in the village of Stratford St Anne.

'We'll put up here, John. A friendly chat with our host

or hostess and an evening keeping our ears open in the taproom will, I trust, prove useful.'

The landlord was an affable fellow who, after shouting for an ostler to see to the horses, showed the travellers into a large taproom with a long table at one end, around which several men sat eating their supper. The room was warm, for in spite of it being so late in the year a wood fire burned in the large fireplace, a spot clearly favoured by the locals who sat on stools in a semi-circle before it. The landlord, appraising Simon's good-quality doublet and lined cloak, assured them he had a room suitable for the gentleman and another for his servant in the attic if that was acceptable. 'And there's pigeon pie followed by a custard for your supper if you so wish. My wife Margery's considered a fine cook.'

The two men seated themselves at the table, greeted their fellow travellers and applied themselves with enthusiasm to the food set before them. After they had eaten Simon nudged John, nodding his head towards the drinkers by the fireside and, as his servant took the hint and made his way over to them, took himself off to a dark corner to observe his progress.

It seems they were to be in luck for a few minutes later the taproom door opened and an elderly man came in, his shoulders draped in sacking, his hands dirty with earth. Without being asked the landlord drew ale into a quart pot and handed it to him. 'Thirsty work, sexton?'

'Ay, it is that.' The sexton thanked him and gave him a coin. 'Let alone having to finish off in the dark.'

'What poor soul is it this time?' enquired one of the

seated drinkers, while his neighbour said that it had been a cruel year and no mistake and he reckoned there'd be more burials to come.

'Harry Pargeter's girl,' replied the sexton. 'Her as went as maid to Miss Olivia up London.' This news immediately stopped all conversation. The sexton, aware he was now the centre of attention, took another long swig from his pot.

'Lord have mercy!' exclaimed the man who had spoken first. 'How did that come about – and her only a young maid!' His neighbour, turning pale, quavered, 'May God preserve us, it's not the Plague, is it, sexton?'

The sexton paused in order to produce the greatest effect. ''Tis not the Plague, neighbour Oats,' he responded with a growing air of importance, 'but 'tis a strange business and no mistake. Seems as the maid was found drowned, floating in Thames river.' At this sensational announcement a number of the drinkers gathered round him, one calling for more ale for the informant, another begging him to continue his tale. Milking every moment, the sexton took several more swigs very slowly before continuing. 'Parson says there was a Crowner's 'quest for fear she took her own life and so couldn't be buried like a Christian soul. But 'twas decided the poor silly girl fell in the water somehow and so drowned.' There was a further buzz of questioning but the sexton would have no more of it. 'More nor that I don't know,' he said firmly, emptying the pot. 'And now I'll home to my bed.'

So this, thought Simon, was to be the received wisdom locally: an unfortunate accident with no rumour of foul play, a nine-days' wonder at most. With the departure of the sexton there was a general move out of the tavern until only a handful of men were left sitting by the fire. Among them was the man addressed as neighbour Oats who, having lost his companion, turned to John, asking him where he came from. John replied comfortably that he and his master (he motioned towards the corner where Simon was sitting) were on their way from London on business. He then offered to buy Oats a drink, adding that the accidental death of so young a girl was a terrible thing.

'If it was an accident,' replied Oats darkly as he took the proffered tankard. 'And the maid didn't take her own life. Crowner's 'quest or no Crowner's 'quest, them in high places like Sir Wolford can see to these things where poor folk can't. When little Jinny Dakin drowned herself for being with child by Sam Berwick two winters gone, she was buried at Four Lanes Cross, poor child. Drove her old mother to the grave herself, it did.'

John nodded sagely, agreeing that money talked. 'And who's this Sir Wolford?' he added.

Oats spat. 'Easy to see you aren't from these parts or you wouldn't need to ask. He owns the old Field estate in the Vale and property up London as well.' Oats was obviously the tavern bore and all too delighted to have found a willing victim.

'A grand old family, I suppose?' prompted John.

Oats was scornful. 'Not him! 'Twas his wife inherited it from her father, old Sir John Field. Now he was real gentry,' he said, settling to his theme. 'Sir John, see, was left with only the one child, both his sons having died young, and this Sir Wolford wanted a fine estate in the country and so took Field's daughter to wife though she was past thirty and plain as a boot. And much good that did him.'

John enquired why.

'Because he's had no son to inherit either, only a daughter he's married off to some lord out of Kent. But he's a very powerful man is Sir Wolford, here and up London too, they say, and does as he likes.' Oats was now getting into his stride. 'As for his daughter, Miss Olivia as was, now there's a strong-willed piece! Always had her own way just like her father, never put to the bridle. If she says Pargeter's girl is to have Christian burial, then her father'll see to it, howsoever the maid drownded.'

'Had the maid a lover then hereabouts?' asked John. 'One that ruined her and wouldn't wed?'

Neighbour Oats thought for a moment. 'She was a good-looking girl in her way and she wasn't short of admirers, but I wouldn't think so. Once she went up to London she thought herself too grand for the likes of the local lads. If she was in that case, then I reckon'd it'd be some rakehell she met in the city.'

Simon watched his servant in deep conversation with some amusement. In circumstances like these John was worth his weight in gold. Seeing things were going well, he rose from his seat and yawned. He was tired and saddle-sore from the ride, and it had been a long day, beginning as it had with old Sara's funeral. Bidding his servant goodnight, he went upstairs. He got undressed, got into bed and blew out his candle. Thinking of Sara's funeral reminded him of the dark and attractive Avisa Allen, her unknowing daughter. He wondered if her husband the silk merchant was one of the thrusting new breed of merchant venturers or an elderly City father happy to acquire an attractive young second wife. He was still pondering on this interesting question when he fell asleep.

From the look of him the next day John Bradedge had drunk deep and late with his companion for by the time he stumbled downstairs his master had already breakfasted. He did, however, manage to recollect most of what he had learned and this he now passed on, adding that he understood the burial was to take place in the first part of the morning. As the taproom windows offered a good view of the churchyard, so making it impossible to miss the funeral party when it arrived, the two men settled down to await the event. Simon, who never travelled without reading matter, sat in the window seat burying himself in *A Compendious Description of Natural Astrology Never to be Briefly Handled Before*, by one John Indagine, Priest, while John fell so heavily asleep in the corner that the maid who was washing the floor gave up trying to wake him up and sloshed her mop around him.

After about half an hour there was noise outside and the rattle of a cart. Simon peered out as it stopped outside the church's lychgate followed by a group of mourners in sombre dress. Four men stepped forward and lifted from it a plain wooden coffin on the lid of which lay a bunch of white flowers tied with white ribbon. They placed the coffin on the slab by the gate as the bell began to toll, first the Six Taylors for the death of a woman, next eighteen strokes for each year of her life, then, as the men shouldered the coffin and began to walk with it towards the grave, the steady death knell.

Without more ado Simon shook John soundly and hauled him, protesting sleepily, out of the door. The path to the church was closely bordered with old yew trees and it was easy to find a vantage point from which they could watch the handful of mourners unseen. The woman in black supported by a young lad whose colouring proclaimed him a relation of Eliza's must surely be her mother. Beside them was a girl of about ten also with the pale family looks and lint-white hair. There were two young women carrying small posies of herbs, whose dress suggested they were servants from the estate, and an older man with an air of authority and importance who was, thought Simon, probably Sir Wolford's steward. As he watched a carriage appeared and also stopped beside the lychgate. The steward at once went over to it, opened the door and deferentially assisted out of it a faded lady in dark grey velvet who was almost certainly Lady Barnes.

As the party approached the graveside they were greeted by the presiding clergyman, a tall, spare figure who, without further preamble, turned and began to intone the first words of the burial service. A brisk breeze blew his words away from where Simon and John were standing and they did not dare move any nearer for risk of being seen but it did seem to Simon that the funeral rite was a short business, over at least as quickly as that of old Sara where there had been no money to pay for anything further. As the coffin was lowered into the grave and those present threw their handfuls of soil and sprigs of flowers on top of it, the young lad, presumably Eliza's brother, left his mother's side and engaged the clergyman in what appeared, from his reaction to them, to be angry words. Indeed it led to an altercation of some kind which ended only when one of the coffin bearers, obviously his father, came over and spoke earnestly to the parson before sweeping his daughter and son away. Meanwhile his wife, after turning to take one last look at the open grave, curtsied to her mistress and followed her family out of the churchyard. Lady Barnes, fussily attended by her steward, then made her way to her carriage making no effort to exchange any courtesies.

For several minutes after the mourners left the clergyman remained by the grave looking thoughtfully after them. Seeing his opportunity, Simon left the shelter of the trees, crossed over towards him and greeted him with a bow.

'Dr Simon Forman, at your service. My apologies, sir, for being here when a burial was taking place. I had been told of your fine old church and having stayed in the village overnight was taking the chance to visit it before returning to London.'

The clergyman returned his courtesy. It was immediately evident that this was no poor churchman standing in for a wealthy incumbent, for his surplice was of superior linen edged with good lace over a long cassock of excellent black cloth. Indeed he had all the appearance of a gentleman. He introduced himself as Dr James Field and agreed that the church was indeed a fine one, adding that the stained glass of the east window was particularly spectacular if Dr Forman would like to see it.

Simon, aware of John still hovering uneasily behind the yews, said he would be most happy to do so after giving instructions to his servant to see to the horses before their return to London that afternoon.

'You are, I take it, Dr Forman, a doctor of medicine and not of divinity like myself?' enquired Field.

'Of Cambridge, sir. And also of Milan.'

The clergyman seemed to make his mind up about something. 'Then I would beg you also to take wine with me afterwards, for I am much in need of advice.'

Chapter 6

A Hundred Guineas

'I suppose I'll have to hang around this dead hole all morning now,' John groused, 'while you chat with the parson.'

Simon grinned. 'I'm sure you can find things to occupy you. I'll find out what he wants to discuss, then see if I can talk to Eliza's family. Tell the landlord we'll be leaving this afternoon and will eat first.' He then rejoined the clergyman who led him into what was certainly a very fine church showing all the marks of having had centuries of wealthy patronage. Simon duly admired the east window, then broached the subject of the burial. 'If I was counting correctly, it seems you buried a mere girl here this morning. It's always a sad business when the young are taken from us.'

Field agreed, then added, 'It was indeed a young woman and it is about that I wish to talk to you.' They left the church passing Eliza's grave where the sexton, assisted by a young lad, was energetically filling it in from the mound of soil beside it, whistling as he worked.

The parsonage was a handsome house with ornate plasterwork and mullioned windows. Once inside it became clear that this was no ordinary country clergyman for the room into which Dr Field led Simon was well furnished, with one wall covered by a large and fine tapestry depicting the Judgement of Solomon. So, thought Simon, Dr James Field must have considerable private means. A pleasant-looking woman appeared asking what her master required and was sent at once for wine. A few minutes later a neatly-dressed maidservant entered with a bottle and two delicate glasses on a silver tray.

Field motioned Simon to take a seat then opened the bottle and poured a glass of red wine. 'You'll find it good, I think. It is sent to me from Bordeaux. You must forgive my not offering you dinner but my wife and daughters are visiting my mother-in-law some miles from here.' He handed the glass to Simon. 'Please excuse my imposing on you in this fashion, Dr Forman, but it is a rare treat to be able to confide in a gentleman such as yourself.'

Simon smiled inwardly at the compliment. He might dress like a gentleman and speak like one but he was well aware that he would never acquire the effortless ease of his host who had been born to it. His right to call himself 'gentleman' was entirely due to his qualification as a physician. It was not his title by right.

Field filled his own glass then abruptly changed the subject. 'Tell me, Dr Forman, is it possible to know from a drowning just how that drowning took place?' Seeing Simon's startled look, he added quickly, 'That is, would it be possible to tell if a person had taken steps to end their life?'

Could it be, thought Simon, that there were others too who had doubts? 'It would be difficult,' he answered cautiously, 'unless the person went into the water from a place so hard to reach that the inference must be that there had been intent. But if you're asking if it's possible to know from a medical point of view how a victim drowned then the answer's no. Unless, that is, there were obvious signs of foul play such as a blow on the head, but that, of course, would be a different matter altogether.'

Field nodded. 'The girl of whom we spoke was pulled out of the Thames some days ago. She was maid to the Lady Olivia Tuckett and all I know is what I learned in the letter she sent me in which she wrote that there had been an Inquest and that the girl did not take her own life. She said also she was unable to leave London to attend the funeral but that her mother would do so and would see I was paid for the burial, the grave and the tolling of the bell. That was all. The girl's parents are decent people and are greatly shocked.'

Simon wondered briefly whether or not to tell him his own view of the matter but decided against it, at least for the time being. He did however enquire why the clergyman was unhappy with what he had been told.

'Because it seemed strange to me that the girl should wander off and simply slip or fall into the water by mischance. You must understand this is not idle conjecture. You see, if there was any question of intent, then I should not have allowed burial in my churchyard. In the circumstances I had little alternative but to accept Lady Tuckett's word, but I am far from satisfied, so much so that I have sent to the Coroner's Office for a copy of the Inquest proceedings. It was because of this I performed only the briefest of rites. It upset the girl's brother very much.' He sighed. 'Put simply, I do not trust Sir Wolford or his family in the very least. If I find out from the Coroner's Office that I have been misled, then it is a most serious matter.'

Simon forbore to comment but in view of his companion's opinion of the Barnes family asked if the incumbency was in the gift of the estate.

The man's reaction was both surprising and unexpected. 'Yes indeed,' he replied bitterly, 'but then the whole estate is mine by right. It is a matter of great dispute. It was left to Sir Wolford in his Will by Sir John Field as part of his daughter's marriage settlement, but in all fairness it should have passed to my branch of the family. My grandfather was Sir John's brother and, there being no son, it should have been inherited first by my father then by myself. My great uncle obviously felt some guilt over the matter since, as the church incumbency was in his gift, he stated it should be given to me when the time came and I had taken my degree and doctorate.' He refilled Simon's wine glass then gave a thin smile. 'However all is not yet quite lost. If the Lady Olivia does not produce a son for Sir Wolford before he dies then it *will* revert to me. Those are the terms of the Will. There is no heir yet but then these are early days and she is not long married.'

He gave Simon a brief resumé of the circumstances leading up to the making of the controversial Will, then turned the conversation to more general topics and they chatted together until the wine was finished. As Simon left, Field told him that he would be welcome to call again if he was ever in the area and observed that next time he came to London he might well seek Simon out. Simon gave him his direction on the Bankside and they parted amicably.

Simon left the rectory in thoughtful mood directed by his host to the Pargeters' cottage. John Bradedge had remembered the history of the Field estate pretty well but his informant had told him nothing of the old squire's Will and may well not have known its terms. So, there had been family conflict over the willing of the estate to Sir Wolford, had there? According to Field his grandfather had been something of a black sheep, a buccaneer on the edge of piracy, although later he settled down into respectable old age having amassed a considerable fortune. Sir John, however, had for years refused to have anything to do with his notorious brother although if fate had not intervened in the shape of Sir Wolford Barnes, he might have softened his stance before he died. It was even possible that this had been in his mind when he had insisted to Sir Wolford's lawyers when the marriage settlement was drawn up that if there should be no male heir before Sir Wolford's death, then the estate would revert back to the family. Sir Wolford had agreed, seeing no reason why he should not father several sons and, in the unfortunate event that there were only daughters, then at the very least there must surely be stout grandsons.

So two families, the Barnes and the Tucketts, were now dependent on Olivia bearing a healthy male child. Meanwhile Dr James Field, rector of St Anne's, rightly incensed that he had most probably lost his inheritance, waited watchfully in the wings; an interesting situation.

A curved drive led up from the main gate of the estate to the fine timbered house which was part of that very inheritance. The sun shone on the long leaded windows while from the formal gardens came the haunting cry of peacocks. The Pargeters' cottage was one of a cluster of small dwellings, almost a hamlet in its own right, which lay to the left of the main house with its stables, dairy, brewery and washhouse.

No one challenged Simon as he passed the lodge and within a few minutes he reached the cottages. It was easy to see which was that of the Pargeters as a wreath of green herbs tied with black ribbon had been fixed to the door. As he was about to knock it was opened by Eliza's brother who was ushering out a small group of people who had evidently been commiserating with the family for they shook him by the hand as they left. All was quiet inside.

Eliza's brother looked somewhat taken aback at the sight of a well-dressed stranger on the doorstep and was starting to shut the door again when Simon stopped him. 'I wonder if I might speak to your parents?' he said. 'I am Dr Simon Forman of London and was passing through on my way to Ipswich when I learned of your sister's death. I've come to pay my respects to your parents, for, you see, I knew her as she consulted me some four months ago.'

The boy stood, unsure what to do, until the delay in closing the door brought his mother to his side. Simon repeated his words and the mother at once motioned her son away and curtsied to him. 'That's very kind of you, sir. Would you be pleased to come in?' The room in which he was shown was neat, clean and sparsely furnished – obviously the best parlour. Through an open doorway he could see a sizeable kitchen from which Eliza's father appeared, now changed back into his work clothes. There was a pervasive smell of clothes dye, for the Pargeters like most working people could not afford special mourning and so had resorted to dying existing garments black. Harry Pargeter stopped short at the sight of Simon. 'This is Dr Forman from London, Harry,' said his wife. 'He tells me our Eliza consulted him some time ago and hearing in the village of our sad trial came to pay his respects.'

Pargeter greeted Simon with some suspicion. 'So you are a doctor, sir? Are you saying then that my daughter came to you because she was sick?'

'No, she wasn't sick,' Simon replied gently, 'she came to ask me to cast her horoscope as many young girls do.'

The news was received with anger. 'Then I must tell you, sir, that I don't hold with such stuff. It's not for Christians to turn to pagan practices to foresee God's will.'

'Now, Harry,' his wife broke in close to tears, 'don't let's have any quarrelling on this of all days. It's likely that Eliza's friends were doing the same and you know how young girls follow each other in fashions.'

'Many physicians use astrological means to aid them in the diagnoses of disease and its outcome,' added Simon. 'It's most respectable, having come to us from the ancients.'

'I still say that's God's business, not man's. So my

daughter wanted nothing more of you?'

'Only a sleeping draught for her mistress.'

'You go off now, Harry, back to your sick mare.' Mistress Pargeter looked at her husband with pity. 'You'll be better back in the stables than sitting here grieving with nothing to do. And you can go back to work too, Joshua,' she said, turning to her son, 'and help comfort your father. We'll expect you both back at dinner time, though as for eating . . .' The tears began once again to trickle down her cheeks.

Pargeter put his arm around her. 'Are you sure you want me to go?'

She nodded and wiped her eyes. 'Leave me be. Grace and I will clear the house and give the doctor some refreshment.' Looking none too sure, her husband kissed her on the cheek then, calling to his son, left the house.

After they had gone Mistress Pargeter invited Simon to take a piece of funeral cake and some ale and then went into the kitchen to fetch them. She was a good-looking woman of a more robust build and warmer colouring than that of Eliza and he imagined that in normal circumstances she would be both brisk and practical. She returned and set a pewter pot of ale and a slice of dark cake before him.

'My lady's told me I don't need to go back to the dairy until tomorrow or even later if I wish, but I expect I will. Like I told Harry, it's best to keep busy and it'll comfort me to be with the other women.' Her voice broke again and hearing this Eliza's sister who had been sitting quietly throughout came over to her mother and held her hand.

'What did you tell our Eliza in her horoscope?' she enquired. 'Did you know something dreadful was going to happen?'

Simon smiled at her in reassurance. 'In truth, I saw nothing bad. Indeed I could learn so little from it that I told her she was quite probably too young for me to be able to cast a reliable horoscope and that perhaps she should come back again when she'd done some more living.'

'That's enough now, Grace,' said her mother patting her arm. 'Go and change your gown, then go back to the kitchen and your spinning wheel. You can think of our poor Eliza while you spin. You are telling us the truth aren't you, Dr Forman?' she asked him as Grace reluctantly left the room. 'If there was something wrong with Eliza, I'd rather know. It can't hurt now.'

Here, thought Simon, was a perceptive woman. 'You speak almost as if you expect there to have been something amiss,' he said.

Mistress Pargeter looked at him for a long moment. 'Since you're a doctor then you must be used to keeping confidences. There's something I'd like to show you. Maybe you can help us throw some light on it.' She went to a cupboard beside the fireplace and brought out a wooden box which she set down on the table. Inside were four small leather bags. She lifted one of them up and shook it gently. There was a chinking sound. ''Tis gold. One hundred guineas in gold.'

Simon stared at her in astonishment. It was an enormous sum.

'I expect Harry would think we should keep it to ourselves but I must tell someone, particularly now that she's . . . she's gone from us. About a month ago, possibly longer, our Eliza came here as the Lady Olivia was up at the house visiting her mother. She showed us the box and told us what was in it and what it was to be used for. Twenty guineas was for Joshua to ensure he was put to a good apprenticeship and could set up in business afterwards – he's just a stable boy working with his father at present. Another twenty was to be set aside as a dowry for Grace. As for the rest, thirty guineas would see Harry and me comfortable well into old age, and the rest was for her own dowry. When I asked her why her portion should be so much more than that of her sister she would say only that there were good reasons.'

'Didn't you question her as to how she'd acquired such wealth?' asked Simon.

'Most certainly. Harry was very worried indeed and kept on trying to make her tell us how it had come to her but she'd say only that it wasn't stolen and no crime had been committed. Harry even made her swear that on the Good Book. She promised him she'd come by it honestly and that it was a gift. But I've never been easy about it in my mind. And now I'm worried to death.'

'And you've still no idea where it came from?'

She hesitated. 'I've wondered since if perhaps she'd been bedded by some wealthy man or young lord and that it was the price of her virginity. For I swear she was a virgin when she entered my lady's service though many good lads here courted her, our neighbours' son John, for one, but our Eliza was cold of nature that way. Though before she left she did say she thought she might now marry and settle down and maybe John would do as well as another. It's passed through my mind that perhaps she found herself with child and that the man who'd taken her had provided for her in this way to help her to a husband, though,' she added bitterly, 'few gentlemen would give so large a sum. As to a husband, young John was certainly fond enough of her and thirty guineas would make most young men agreeable to such a match, child or no child, especially if she wasn't too far forward and it might decently be passed off as her husband's. So that's why I asked if the horoscope was the real reason she consulted you in case you were trying to spare us.'

Simon shook his head. 'No, I spoke truly. She did come for a horoscope and poppy syrup for her mistress and I can tell you for certain that she couldn't have been with child then.'

She understood the nuance straight away. 'What are you saying?'

'That she was, though, some three months' forward when she died. It fell to me to help take her body from the river and I examined her,' said Simon.

Mistress Pargeter turned pale. 'So she could have drowned herself after all?'

'It's possible, mistress, but I don't believe so. The truth has been kept from you. I will tell you now that I saw her body and am convinced she was constrained in some manner before she entered the river and went to her death. The verdict of the Crowner's 'quest was wilful murder.'

'Sweet Jesus!' the woman replied. 'Dear God in Heaven! We've been told nothing except that she didn't drown herself. So she *was* with child? If you're right, was that the reason for this, do you think? But why should anyone do such a terrible thing?'

'I don't know, Mistress Pargeter,' said Simon. 'But I intend to do everything I can to find out. In the meantime, I think it might be best if you keep this knowledge to yourself for the present. That is if you feel strong enough.'

She lifted her head. 'I will have to be. I can't think what Harry and Joshua might do if they had any such notion, and the good Lord alone knows what will happen when they do find out.' As Simon left she pressed his hand in silent gratitude. 'You've been most kind, sir. It's rare for a man in your position to take such an interest.'

'Believe me,' he told her, 'I won't rest myself until I get to the bottom of this matter. When I learn more, I'll send you word.'

Half an hour later Mistress Pargeter was surprised to find Sir Wolford's steward at her door. Matthew Laurence was a self-important, officious man, much disliked by the rest of the servants, not least because little happened on the estate without his knowledge, which he passed on to his master. Mistress Pargeter had little alternative but to ask him in and was starting to say that she would be back in the dairy the next morning when he stopped her.

'That's for you to decide, as my lady told you. But that's not why I'm here. I'm told you've had a visitor. A man from London. May I ask who he was and why he called on you this day of all days?'

She wondered how he had learned of it so quickly. Someone had been busy. 'He was a doctor, Master Laurence. A Dr Simon Forman. It seems he was staying in the village by chance and, hearing of our Eliza's death, came to pay his respects since she'd once consulted him in London.' Even if Simon had not warned her, her dislike of the steward was such that she would not have elaborated further.

'I see. And did he tell you why she called on him?'

'He said she'd come for medicine for Lady Olivia and also, like so many foolish girls, because she wanted her horoscope cast.'

The steward considered this. 'And that was all?'

'What more could there be?'

The steward regarded her in silence. 'And you say this doctor's name was Forman?'

Mistress Pargeter nodded and showed him out.

On his return to the house Laurence immediately took pen and paper and swiftly penned a note to his master after which, calling a servant, he told the man he wanted it taken at once to Sir Wolford in London, breaking his journey on the way only if he must.

Chapter 7

The Lady in Grey

The weary messenger duly arrived at Sir Wolford's home the next morning and, after some argument with the porter at the gate, was shown in to the house. Sir Wolford, always testy at the start of the day, was far from pleased to be told an urgent message had arrived from the country, but the contents of the letter made him send at once for his secretary. Eliza's fate had been of such little interest to him that he had not even thought to enquire as to the result of the Inquest. The girl was dead, had been taken home to be buried, and that was that. If he thought about it at all it was only to be thankful that a valuable piece of jewellery had been retrieved along with her body. He was, therefore, irritated to be reminded of the affair.

As Francis Down entered the room he thrust the letter at him and demanded an explanation, pacing up and down in annoyance. 'What's the meaning of it?' he growled as Down cast his eye at the steward's letter. 'This Dr Forman. Wasn't he the man who came here and told us of the girl's death?'

Down agreed that it was.

'Then what in the Devil's name is he doing prowling around my estate?'

According to Master Laurence's letter, he told Mistress Pargeter he was in Stratford St Anne by chance,' replied Down smoothly. 'But if you want my opinion, then I would suggest he was there by design and for some purpose of his own.'

'And what might that be? And why is he meddling in my affairs?'

'Perhaps, sir, you've not heard what transpired at the Inquest?'

'Heard what, man? Get to the point in God's name. This tale will outlast a night in Russia where the nights are long.'

Down assumed his silkiest tone. 'That, thanks to Dr Forman, the verdict on Eliza was one of wilful murder.'

Sir Wolford was so amazed he stopped in his tracks. 'Have you taken leave of your senses?'

'Dr Forman spoke of marks on the girl's wrists,' Down continued, 'marks he said had been made by ropes which must have been used to restrain her. There were other signs also that led him to believe she'd been done to death and the jury reluctantly agreed, although the Coroner was far from happy about it. I can only think, therefore, that Forman went to the Vale to see if he could discover anything which might help support his theory.'

'The man's an impertinent menace!' boomed Sir Wolford.

Down agreed, 'Quite so.'

'So what are we to do about it?' bellowed his master, 'before he sets not only the whole town by the ears with his tale but the country folk as well?'

'If you will hear me out, sir,' Down replied, 'I think there are two things that can be done to prevent his causing you any more trouble. First, when I told your daughter of the verdict she informed me that Eliza had once confided in her that she'd taken a violent lover, who sometimes beat her. Your daughter, out of concern for the girl, pleaded with her to give him up. If Dr Forman is right, therefore, it would seem she refused to heed Lady Olivia's advice. If it's true that she suffered some kind of assault before being put into the river, then surely that man is the most obvious person to have done the deed. Maybe she was even intending to give him the stolen pendant, only they quarrelled fatally before she could do so.'

Sir Wolford considered this. 'Does Olivia know this fellow's name?'

'I don't believe so. She said only that he was a seafarer of some kind. No doubt by now he's safely on his way to the other side of the world.'

'Well, that's something,' responded Sir Wolford. 'So what does this have to do with Dr Forman?'

'I suggested to your daughter that she wrote to the coroner, telling him of the situation and explaining that she had been too upset to inform him of it before the Inquest. She might also say that she would like Dr Forman to be told, as he is proving himself a nuisance. That should settle the matter where the Coroner's Office is concerned.'

'And has Olivia written to him?'

'I haven't enquired.'

'Then let's find out,' said Sir Wolford. 'Go and tell her I must see her immediately.'

He waited with increasing impatience until Down returned, only to be informed that Lady Olivia had gone out.

'Very well then. *I'll* write to the coroner! Or rather you will and I'll sign it. Do it now. I presume he attends the Inns of Court? Have it sent round straight away.' Sir Wolford paused. 'Did you say there was also a second way of dealing with Forman?'

Down smiled. 'I've made it my business to make enquiries about him. On your behalf,' he added hastily. 'And I've discovered that he's not well thought of by the Royal College of Physicians. He's a nobody who has come from nowhere and he had a good deal of trouble convincing the Royal College that he was properly qualified. Indeed, they've called him before their Council on a number of occasions, one senior doctor going so far as to tell me he thought the man a notorious imposter. For some time they refused to grant him a licence to practise.'

'Is he not a proper physician than?' asked Sir Wolford.

'He claims to have trained in Italy and it seems that in the end he was able to persuade the University of Cambridge to recognise him and so the College was forced to agree also. But there are many there who would be only too happy to see his licence withdrawn. Surely, therefore, a doctor who meddles in the affairs of others, affairs which have nothing to do with medicine, is deserving of being brought to their attention? Particularly as he has also recently upset a distinguished coroner. A judicious complaint to the Royal College might well result in his no longer being able to practise.'

Sir Wolford rubbed his hands. 'You've done well, Down, very well. Write another letter to the physicians and send that off too. I won't tolerate anyone, anyone, interfering in my affairs!'

Simon and John clattered back into London the next morning, having spent the night at an inn some fifteen miles outside the city. As was ever the case when he had been away, half the local population seemed to have been struck ill and decided to consult Simon, the apothecary he used most often had been back twice to know the ingredients for a certain medicine for the shingles and was even now awaiting his return in the kitchen, and, Anna informed Simon, a lady in grey had called the previous afternoon and, finding him away from home, had returned again that morning. She had refused to leave her name.

His first task was to give the apothecary the list of ingredients for the draught to soothe the shingles; plantain leaves boiled in barley water to which, after it was strained, was added powdered orris root, Armenian bole and a little ground bloodstone. The apothecary made a careful note and thanked him. While Simon made up many of his own remedies the apothecary both sought his advice and kept in his store larger amounts of some draughts and ointments and their ingredients than Simon was able to do, which he provided Simon with ready-made. Like most of his craft, the apothecary both supplied physicians and prescribed himself, especially to those too poor or too frightened to consult a doctor.

'There's much scurvy too, Doctor, after the bad weather. What do you think best?'

'If it's only slight they should eat watercress. I take it you tell them that or give it to them boiled with scurvy grass and frumentary?'

'Aye,' said the apothecary, 'but in many cases it still persists.'

'Then try agrimony, liquorice and rhubarb boiled with waters of wormwood and cinnamon. What they need most, though, is a fine summer and there's precious little sign of that.' The apothecary thanked Simon and left.

His venture into Essex had left Simon with much to think about. He found it impossible to believe that Eliza's extraordinary hoard of guineas did not play some part in the story. As to Dr James Field and his usurped inheritance, he was unable to decide whether this had any relevance or not. Had it been Olivia who had been found in the Thames then possibly the urbane clergyman might have been suspected of having some hand in it, although Simon felt he was now moving into the realms of a tale in the playhouse, but Field could hardly gain anything from murdering her maid. It was all very difficult.

At this point Anna came to tell Simon that the lady in grey had returned and was demanding to see him straight away. She had been shown into his study. As he washed his hands in the kitchen, Simon toyed with the possibility that the dark and enticing Avisa had found him as interesting as he had her and had come to consult him as a consequence.

When he opened the door of his study the girl in grey was standing on the same spot and in almost the same attitude as on that first occasion and for a moment his blood turned chill. But it was no restless wraith called back from the dead. The height and build, even the stance, were almost identical, but it was not Eliza Pargeter. Olivia Tuckett's hair was a darker gold, her pale grey gown of fine velvet. He greeted her formally, then offered her a chair, asking if she would be seated. They sat opposite to one another, the desk between them. He wondered why she was there.

'I'm sorry I was from home when you called earlier,' he said.

She shrugged. 'I came on chance but as you see I'm here now.' She began without further preamble. 'You seem to have brought about a great deal of unnecessary trouble, Dr Forman. I would have thought you'd had enough to divert you without involving yourself in the death of my maid.'

He had to admire her frankness. 'I fear I don't under-stand,' he replied. 'Perhaps you'll be so good as to enlighten me as to what trouble I'm alleged to have caused, Lady Tuckett. It was purely by chance that your maid's body was brought to the watersteps beside my house. Having been presented with it, I informed the Coroner's Office and examined it as I would any other in such circumstances.'

'But you went further, didn't you?' she continued. 'Telling the Inquest that you believe she was murdered?'

'That is indeed my belief. Based on medical evidence

from the injuries she had sustained. As you will know it appears the jury agreed with me.'

Olivia got up from her chair, obviously too restless to sit still. 'It is a great pity you did not come to me first and tell me what you proposed to say. There are matters on which I could have enlightened you.'

He wondered what was to come next. 'Then pray do so now, Lady Tuckett.'

She inclined her head. 'Very well. Had you asked, then I could have told you that for many months Eliza had had a violent lover who sometimes beat her, and on the night of her death she had an assignation with this man. I only realised she was missing on the morning of the day she was found in the river, because I had passed the previous evening in Blackfriars with my friend Celia Wynter – her father and mine are colleagues – and I had returned much later than expected, having been overcome with a sudden bout of faintness. It being past midnight by the time I arrived at my father's house, I naturally assumed, since Eliza wasn't in my chamber, that she had retired to bed. I saw no point in disturbing her.

'I had warned her against this lover many times but she took no heed. Possibly she was one of those who find enjoyment in being subjected to pain. You must know that there are such women – and indeed men. It would seem, therefore, that if your theory is right then it is this man you should be seeking.'

Simon lent back in his chair. 'I see. Certainly there's no end to the strange practices to which some men and women resort to take their pleasure, but I don't believe

Eliza Pargeter was one of them. I'm willing to swear that when she came to see me she'd never had a lover, violent or otherwise. From what she asked it was clear that she'd had no carnal knowledge of men – then. Later, of course, she must have taken a man since she was with child. But not, I think, by a violent lover. Now, if that is all you have come to say, then I beg you to excuse me for I've many demands on my time, having been out of my practice for the best part of three days.'

Olivia swung round. 'But that's not all. I've also come to consult you professionally. You are, after all, a physician.'

'How can I help you then?'

'It seems I cannot conceive. I've been married now for several months but there is still no child.'

Simon smiled. 'That's a very short time, my lady. While there are those who deliver their first child nine months to the day after the wedding night, there are many who must wait longer: months or even years. Your courses are regular?'

She nodded.

'And your relations with your husband are satisfactory?'

She stamped her foot. 'Satisfactory? How shall I reply to that? If you mean have I set my teeth and allowed his crude gropings and slavering kisses, followed by two minutes of coupling (when he is not too drunk to rise to the occasion) as is the duty of a wife, then yes, I've done my duty. But satisfactory? As well be satisfied by a night in a sty with a pig?'

Simon stifled a smile, then said, 'I merely meant were

you having normal carnal relations with your husband? I took care not to describe them as the act of love. But what I've told you is true. It's early days. However, if you wish, I can make you up a draught which might help.'

'Very well.' She watched him as he went over to his shelves to find the necessary herbs. Then she came over to him, again standing close enough for him to smell her perfume. She really was, he thought, looking into those strange dark eyes, a most dangerously attractive woman. His thoughts must have shown in his face as for the first time she smiled at him. Then her mood changed. 'If a woman has once rid herself of a child, might she then be unable to conceive?'

'Are you telling me that you've previously been with child and made away with it?'

She bit her lip. 'I presume you say nothing of what passes in this room? Then yes, some two years ago I found myself in such a pass.'

'And what did you do?'

'I went to see a woman near St Paul's. You must know that such things are common knowledge even among women of my station.'

'And did she give you a draught or use an instrument on you?'

'She gave me a draught. It was bitter,' Olivia grimaced at the memory. 'Then she laid a plaster on my stomach and the next day, as she promised, the pains started. As soon as I had left her I travelled to the country with Eliza who tended me throughout. It was terrible. I thought I'd die.'

'And might well have done so,' said Simon. 'As well as being evil, it's very dangerous indeed. You might bleed to death. Also very foolish, which I wouldn't have supposed you to be. As to preventing conception, then yes, it's possible that some damage has occurred which might prevent what you so much desire.'

'I see.' She looked thoughtful then shook her head as if she were trying to put the possibility out of her mind. 'Tell me, Dr Forman, if you don't think me foolish, what do you suppose me to be?' She held his eyes in a long look.

'Clever and dangerous,' he answered, 'and now here is your draught. For two weeks you must drink as much as will go into a small spoon each night before you retire and we'll see if it proves to be of benefit.' She took the green glass phial and stowed it carefully in the pocket hanging from her gown from which she now took some coins. 'I'll take two florins from you, my lady, for you can afford my services while many who need me more cannot.'

She paid him without demur. 'They say many things of you, Dr Forman. That you're a necromancer who has a pact with the Devil and can raise spirits. But that I do not believe. They also say you alone have the secret of recovering from the Plague.'

'That's no secret. I've a strong constitution and took to my bed with my own medicines and cut the buboes when they appeared with a clean instrument.'

They moved towards the door. 'Are you married?' she asked suddenly.

'I am not,' he replied with a vehemence which surprised himself.

'I only asked. Has no lady taken your fancy sufficiently then?'

'I did not say that.'

She smiled mischievously. 'You are perhaps of the other persuasion? Don't look so taken aback. It was well regarded in the days of the Ancient Greeks and there are many such. It is said that the Rose poet, Christopher Marlowe, is one such.'

In spite of himself he smiled back. 'You can take my word for it that I am not.'

She laughed. 'I will confess I have been having a joke with you. For I must tell you that I've heard that some women who consult you find you so sympathetic that they pay you in kind. Perhaps we might negotiate such an arrangement if the medicine fails? Who knows, you might furnish me with an heir.'

What game was she playing now, Simon asked himself. 'You might still be disappointed – in every way,' he replied. 'In the meantime take the draught I've given you and let's hope it succeeds.'

'One way and another, I must succeed in this,' she said, as he placed her cloak around her shoulders. 'Too much hangs on it to be otherwise. I must go, I've kept you from your patients long enough. And forget Eliza, Dr Forman. Believe me, there's no further point in pursuing the matter.'

He opened the front door for her and Olivia swept out without a backward glance, leaving him staring thoughtfully after. He returned to his study, pausing in the doorway to remember how for a brief instant he had thought her to be Eliza's ghost. It was then a fantastic thought struck him.

Chapter 8
Poppy Syrup

Olivia left Simon's house in thoughtful mood, followed by the bored servant who had spent his time yawning outside, wishing his mistress had been of a mind to suggest he wait for her in a tavern. The Bankside was no place for a lady of quality on foot and he carried a stout stick in case of trouble. She walked at a brisk pace, hardly noticing her surroundings, her mind returning to the ingenious idea that had started the whole ill-fated train of events.

So deep in thought was she that she almost walked by her own gate. Her arrival brought her reverie to an end. She had risen early leaving Marcus, as was usual, snoring in their bed reeking of stale wine, and had found little difficulty in slipping out of the house that morning without being seen. She assumed she was unlikely to have been missed as her father would be busy with his own affairs and as for Marcus, they lived as separate lives as was possible while still remaining under one roof.

Dr Forman's earlier absence had meant that she had stayed out longer than intended but she was quite unprepared for the reception that greeted her. First she was told by an agitated maid that her father had been looking for her all morning and had told the servants to send her to him immediately she returned. Next, scarcely had she handed her cloak to the girl and started out in search of Sir Wolford but Marcus appeared, booted and spurred and obviously ready to go on a journey. A message had come from his home to say that his father had suffered some kind of seizure the previous day and therefore he was leaving at once to see if it was serious. He trusted he would not be away for long, he told her, but if it was necessary for him to remain in Kent for any length of time, then he expected her to join him.

Olivia made some non-committal reply. She heartily disliked the Tuckett household in Kent. Marcus's mother had died years before and that, coupled with the fact that both father and son had squandered their income, meant that for years everything had been grossly neglected. The roof of the once grand house leaked, there was damp everywhere, the floors were flea-ridden, the tapestries rotted where they hung. Bad masters made bad servants and the service was surly and grudging. Used as she was to the comfort of her City home and the orderly house in Essex she found it intolerable. She counted herself fortunate that Marcus loathed the country, much preferring life in London. She bade him farewell, politely sent her best wishes to his father for a swift recovery and finally continued on her way to her own.

She found Sir Wolford poring over ledgers with Francis Down. He looked up as she entered the room, grunted a greeting and asked irritably where she'd been.

'I merely went out to choose some silk for a new gown,' she told him, 'and then on to the ruff-maker to ask her to make me one in the new fashion starched with yellow starch.'

'You took long enough about it,' he grumbled. 'Anyway now you're here perhaps you can tell me why I wasn't informed of the verdict of the Crowner's 'quest on your girl, Eliza?'

'You've been busy, Father, and, if you recall, you told me very definitely when Dr Forman came to tell us of her death that it was for me to deal with as it was my concern, not yours. I therefore saw no reason to worry you with it.'

The mention of the name Forman caused Sir Wolford to let loose a string of oaths he rarely used in front of his family: God's blood, but the man was a menace, a meddling charlatan who had somehow bewitched the jury into coming up with a rubbishy verdict no one would believe in order to denigrate the Barnes's household. Sir Wolford then went on in direct contradiction to what he had just said to ask Olivia if she had written to the coroner, as Francis Down had suggested, telling him of the girl's involvement with a violent lover. She replied that she had not yet had time.

'It's as well then,' he snapped, 'that there's been someone to do it for you. When Down told me of it, I immediately sent a letter to Monkton this morning myself informing him.'

'If that's what's made you so angry, then I'm sorry and admit I was remiss in not doing so but surely all that matters is that a letter has now been sent.'

'It's not all that matters, my girl. Do you know Forman's been down to Stratford St Anne? Laurence actually discovered he'd had the temerity to poke about there. It seems he spent a considerable time with James Field and, more to the point, visited the Pargeters on the very day of the funeral.'

This did surprise her but she did not show it, merely asking if her father knew why he had done so.

Sir Wolford made a gesture of impatience. 'How should I? Laurence wrote he got nothing out of Field and that Mistress Pargeter told him only that Forman's story was that he just happened to be passing through the village that day, learnt of her daughter's death and therefore came to pay his respects. But don't tell me it was by chance! For whatever reason, he quite obviously went down deliberately to poke about, though what he was expecting to find I can't imagine. Anyway it's all going to stop thanks to Down here.' He nudged his secretary. 'Tell Olivia what we have done.'

For a split second she wondered if her father and Down had decided to make away with Simon Forman as she had once begged Down to do. She found she no longer wanted this to happen unless there was no other possible alternative. Francis Down smiled at her, holding her eyes as if he knew what she was thinking.

'I told your father, my lady, that I'd discovered that for a host of reasons Dr Forman is much disliked and distrusted by the Royal College of Physicians who only granted him a licence to practise after considerable pressure from the University of Cambridge. In fact there are those who consider him little better than a charlatan. I've therefore written to the College on your father's behalf informing them that Dr Forman has been acting in a way which must throw discredit on the entire profession by meddling in matters which have nothing to do with him and which have grossly offended Sir Wolford. Also that he has annoyed a distinguished coroner by making wild allegations which persuaded a jury to bring in a verdict other than that the coroner thought appropriate, thus involving this household in a most unsavoury affair. Sir Wolford trusts, therefore, that they will take immediate action with regard to Dr Forman.'

'They'd better!' broke in Sir Wolford. 'I'll not rest until the scoundrel's lost his livelihood. What do you say, Olivia?'

'You certainly seem to have everything in hand, Father, so unless you want me for anything further, there are domestic affairs I must see to. Marcus, as you probably know, has gone down to Kent as Lord Tuckett's been taken ill.'

'Off you go then. I suppose,' Sir Wolford added, 'that if old Tuckett dies you'll have to spend much of your time in Kent. There should be enough domestic affairs down there to keep you fully occupied.' He turned back to his ledgers and Olivia, avoiding Down's eye, left to go about her business.

Even though Lady Barnes rarely spent much time in London, hers was a well-run household. The cook, with whom Olivia now discussed dishes for that day and the next, was an excellent one, while a capable housekeeper saw to it that her master's home was kept in a manner suitable for a merchant venturer who regularly entertained fellow merchants from both home and abroad. Having seen that everything was in order, Olivia returned restlessly to her own sitting room in a state of turmoil. She considered she'd dealt with Simon Forman rather well. He really was a very attractive man and her provocative offer had not been entirely in jest. She wondered why he had reacted so strongly when she'd asked him if he had a wife. She had left him hoping she had succeeded in persuading him of her own alibi and that there was nothing more to gain from pursuing the matter of Eliza's death any further, but if that indeed was the case, then her father's actions, egged on by Francis Down, were bound to stir up the hornets' nest all over again.

The next morning, having received no night summonses and without any waiting patients, Simon decided to check through his medicines, salves and herbs to see what he might need to buy either from the apothecary or from the importers of herbs, spices and mineral ingredients. The poor weather had set his own garden herbs back weeks and those he had dried the previous summer were fast losing their strength. He was meticulous about such things and once involved he settled down to do the job properly, telling Anna that she could clean each shelf as he cleared it, which she was happy to do as usually he did not allow her to touch any of the jars or boxes.

As he lifted the lids and stoppers of the jars and peered into them, automatically checking their contents and jotting down any necessary ingredient as he went along, his mind endlessly circled around Eliza's hundred guineas;

so vast a sum for a young servant girl. The obvious possibility was surely that she was being paid to hold her tongue. No doubt the Barnes household like most others had its secrets but if that was the case then the sheer size of the sum involved suggested something extraordinarily serious and he wondered what on earth it could be.

So, if she'd embarked on such a course, who then had she approached? Olivia was the most obvious choice but why would Eliza risk jeopardising a position many girls from her background would consider most enviable?

Had she, therefore, been more ambitious and tried her hand on Sir Wolford himself or even Marcus Tuckett? Eliza, sharp as a needle, had been well placed to pick up secrets – but again he'd have thought her too shrewd to make so blatant a use of any embarrassing knowledge she might have as she must realise that if her demand for money was rejected, she risked being turned out of the household at best, with no references or hope of another position, and at worst accused on some trumped-up charge of being dishonest or mad. If the latter then she would end up either in Bridewell prison or the madhouse.

There was also the question of the child she was carrying. Who was its father? Someone in the household? If so then the most she could have expected was to be modestly paid off if it were a member of the family or married off if it was one of the servants. He thought again of the remarkable superficial likeness between the two young women. It was a preposterous idea but could it be that somehow and for some reason, either by chance or design, they'd been mistaken for each other? What if Eliza had been killed by someone thinking she was Olivia? But if that was the case surely the murderer would have realised his mistake before it was too late.

Simon felt totally confused. It was at this point that he reached the back row of jars on the second shelf and discovered that half a jar of poppy syrup was missing. He held it up to the light and peered at it. Surely he couldn't have forgotten prescribing so much? He showed the jar to Anna who stopped briefly in her labours, shook her head and shrugged. Surely John would never have . . . ? Shouting loudly, Simon went in search of his man and found him seeing to a saddle in the yard.

'Do you know anything about a missing half-jar of poppy juice?' he demanded.

John's guilty expression was enough. Roaring with rage, Simon took him by the collar, hauled him into the house and pushed him into the study where the offending jar stood on the desk. He then released him, stood back, and pointed at it. One look at his master's face told John there was serious trouble ahead. He started to speak but Simon took no notice.

'Spare me any excuses. It has to be you for no one else, so far as I'm aware, has spent sufficient time in here alone to have been able to steal half the contents and make off with them, let alone find a jar in which to carry the stuff away.'

Anna remained looking totally nonplussed as well she might, but John, now recognising there was no help for it, admitted that he had indeed taken some of it, 'But only on your orders, sir.'

'On my orders? What on earth do you mean? My orders are, and always have been, that you never, never prescribe anything yourself.'

'I know that,' replied his unhappy servant, 'but she was so very definite about it. How she'd been on her way to see you but, meeting you outside St Paul's and you in haste, you'd told her to come here and ask me to give her the poppy syrup in your place. I did press her several times to make sure that's what you'd told her but she said again and again that—'

'Who said? Who is this woman whose word you chose to take over mine?'

John gulped. 'It was her, Dr Forman. The girl, Eliza. She who's now dead.'

Simon looked at him in so appalled a fashion that John felt sick to the pit of his stomach. Visions formed in his mind of himself, Anna and baby Simon being turned out on to the street forthwith. Simon regarded him grimly. 'Come outside with me,' he said, his voice quivering with rage, then added to Anna, 'continue cleaning the shelves if you will, this obviously has nothing to do with you.'

Once outside he exploded. 'As for you – you – poltroon, you lackwit, perhaps you'd now be good enough to tell me exactly what happened?'

John limped out his story. How Eliza had arrived saying that the doctor had told her to come to him for the sleeping medicine, how he'd meant to tell his master what he'd done – he really had – but somehow what with one thing and another he'd almost forgotten about it until Eliza had been hauled out of the river.

'And when precisely was this?' queried Simon.

John thought a little then said he reckoned it'd been a week or so after her second visit. 'Yes, that's right. Come to think of it, she said so. She said you'd told her to come back for more if she needed it and the first bottle didn't cure her mistress's sleeplessness. I suppose she must have stood outside somewhere waiting for you to go out. She gave me a good fee, half a sovereign. I put it in your poorbox,' he added hoping this virtuous deed might assist. 'I know I shouldn't really have done it, Doctor, but she did seem to know what she was about. And I didn't do any harm, did I?'

Simon banged his hand down on a nearby chest, realising as pain shot up his arm that it was the injured one. It did nothing to put him in a better humour. 'Oh, she knew what she was about all right. I can well believe it. As to harm, God's breath, man, you gave her enough poppy juice to put a troop of horses to sleep! Don't you realise,' he continued, warming to his theme, 'that selling her the poppy syrup almost certainly led to her death? At the very least you gave those who made away with her the means of rendering her insensible while they tied her up and threw her in the river!'

John could find nothing to say except to mumble yet again how sorry he was. Simon looked at him in exasperation. On the whole John was a good and useful servant to have about the place, while Anna kept his house as clean and neat as a new pin. The man had made a foolish, possibly fatal, mistake but he could well believe that Eliza had been as convincing as John said she was.

'All right, all right,' Simon said with a resigned sigh. 'We'll leave it there now. But let this be a lesson to you for the future. If it ever happens again there'll be no second chance.'

Chastened, John withdrew rapidly to his refuge in the yard while Simon returned to his study shaking his head in disbelief. He might have been exaggerating when he'd said Eliza had taken away enough poppy syrup to knock out a troop of horses but there was certainly enough to do a great deal more mischief; and most of it, presumably, was still in the possession of Olivia Tuckett.

Chapter 9

The Council of Physicians

Simon spent most of the day following his discovery of the missing poppy juice casting round to see if there was anything that could be done about it. Should he tackle Olivia Tuckett directly, pointing out that so large an amount was dangerous and that she should return to him any that was now left? But she might well reply either that she had never sent Eliza for it in the first place and therefore knew nothing of it or, that if she had, then it had been paid for and was rightfully hers. He had always been exceptionally careful when it came to prescribing medicines. He knew that many doctors did not worry too much about what they gave their patients, many of whom they would see either infrequently or never again, and there were plenty of quack doctors about too and others with only the most minimal knowledge, with no formal qualifications, who set up in practice as and where they could and whose potions often did more harm than good. And now this had happened to him who recorded every case, every medicine or salve he prescribed, in his Casebook.

The next morning was a busy one with a succession of people knocking at his door from eight o'clock onwards.

There was a woman with two children, both of whom had ringworm, for which he gave her a powder made of the herb savin, pointing out that it most likely grew in her garden and could be dried for future use. Next a workman with boils for whom he prescribed barberries boiled in white wine; then a sloe-eyed young married woman who wanted her horoscope cast. Last of all was Thomas Pope, an actor in the company of the Lord Admiral's Men based in the nearby Rose Theatre. Theatre people often came to Simon for advice, not only because he lived among them but also because he was a keen playgoer and was therefore on familiar terms with many actors and their families.

'It's easy to see what's wrong with you, my friend!' he said as Pope entered his study, his eyes streaming, his nose red.

'I doubt it's as easy to cure though,' replied the actor, his voice reduced to a thin croak. 'It's this wretched weather. It gets so cold in the theatre standing around and the damp doesn't do one's voice any good at all. Henslowe,' he added, 'was threatening to dose me himself.'

Philip Henslowe, timber merchant, builder, bear-warden, entrepreneur extraordinary and also owner of the Rose Theatre, was notorious for fancying himself as a doctor and prescribing his own gruesome cures to members of his company. His eagerness to try out his skill in this field usually meant that the mere threat of being dosed with one of his brews either caused the prospective recipient to make a startling and immediate recovery or, if that was impossible, to send him round hotfoot to the nearest physician.

'Well, you know as well as I do,' said Simon, 'that there's precious little that can be done about the rheum except to let it take its course, but I'll do my best to ease you.' He searched among his bottles, selected two jars and set out two phials, one larger than the other. He then filled them both. 'The first is a draught of liquorice and can be taken throughout the day. It will help to stem the streaming. The other, which should be mixed with wine and is for your sore throat, is what they call Saracen's woundwort, a mighty herb which comes under the influence of Saturn and can be used for all manner of conditions. As its name suggests, it was brought back to us by the Crusaders as was the juice of the white poppy . . .' He stopped, suddenly reminded of the missing sedative. It gave him an idea.

'Sit a minute if you will, Thomas,' Simon said, 'for I'd rather like to consult you. I'll give you a glass of the woundwort in wine to ease you as we speak. Tell me,' he asked as he poured the mixture into the glass and handed it to the actor, 'are there many plays in which a mistress changes places with her maid?'

Pope thought for a moment. 'There are some old comedies though none we play ourselves. Such stories go back to the days of the old Roman dramatists but if I remember rightly there are similar plots in the merry tales of Boccaccio.'

'And the reasons why such an exchange takes place?'

'Oh, the usual. So that the mistress can escape from the home of her father or husband to meet a lover. There's also what we call the "bed-switch" plot in which one girl, not necessarily a maid, is substituted for another on the wedding night either because the bridegroom's jilted her after the formal betrothal and she should really have been his wife, or because she loves him whereas the real bride doesn't. Personally I think it a silly story since I find it most unlikely a man could be so fooled in real life. I would never have thought some other girl my Jenny on our wedding night; I'd have needed to have been insensible!'

He smiled at this. He and Jenny were noted for their devotion to each other. He warmed to his theme. 'There are far more stories, of course, in which master and man take each other's part so that the master can woo the girl of his choice in disguise, while the man carries off his master's part in society so that none is the wiser. There's such a plot in the old play of the shrewish bride tamed by her bridegroom.' He paused. 'You've given me an idea. Perhaps we could get one of our new young lions of the theatre to rewrite that one. I'll mention it to Henslowe.'

Simon looked thoughtful. 'But could it not be, if much was at stake, that if such an exchange between mistress and maid took place the maid would become a hazard to her mistress? That from then on she would be a threat?'

'You're talking now of intrigue and tragedy, not comedy,' responded Pope. 'It sounds more like the plot of an Italian or Spanish piece than anything we have in our repertoire at the Rose.' He looked at Simon with sudden interest. 'Are you suggesting such a thing has actually happened? In real life?'

Simon had always liked Pope and was also desperate to confide in someone. 'Please keep this to yourself but yes, I'm not sure but I think it might have done. Though I can't see how or why. It's just a feeling I have. But whether or not it actually happened, the lady's maid is now dead, pulled from the river some days ago with rope marks on her wrists.'

Pope whistled through his teeth. 'Now *there's* a plot for a drama! Perhaps I should suggest that too, just as an idea, of course: "The True Tragedy of the Murdered Substitute"!' Then he stopped as a sudden thought struck him. 'Are you talking about the girl found here a week or so ago? I was with members of the company in the Anchor the night after the Inquest and the potboys were full of the fact that the verdict was wilful murder. How very unpleasant. If anything further occurs to me I'll drop over and let you know, but I suppose I'd better get back to work before Henslowe insists on dosing me with ground worms in boys' urine or some such.' He stood up. 'Your medicine's eased my throat but I still can't see how it's going to be possible to get my voice to carry this afternoon.'

'Can't you rest up for a couple of days? You'll risk straining it further as it is.'

'You know what Henslowe's like where money's concerned. He rarely has actors who can stand in when one of us is sick. It's *Tamburlaine* again today. I'm supposed to convince an audience that I'm that "mighty man at arms" ready to join Tamburlaine and "triumph over all the world" when all I can manage is a faint squeak. The groundlings will eat me!' On which note he departed.

The conversation with Pope left Simon feeling restless.

If his tentative theory was right and Eliza and Olivia had changed places for some reason then it raised many questions, but most crucial being why it had been necessary and why Eliza had agreed to it. The obvious answer to the latter question was for money, although it might also have been done out of loyalty or even coercion. As to the reason for it . . . Had Olivia risked a lover around the time of her marriage and had disguised herself as Eliza? Which led him on to ponder on Olivia's unwanted child and its putative father.

He must surely have been someone she knew her family would consider totally unsuitable as a husband or the matter could have been easily rectified, with the added bonus that Sir Wolford was desperately in need of a male heir. The marriage of an expectant bride was hardly uncommon and the fashion for large farthingales and spreading skirts allowed easy concealment. As to the time of the birth of the child, he'd seen a fair number of supposedly seven-months' infants whose size and development belied what was claimed to have been the date of their conception.

Maybe, after all, the idea that had come to him when for a moment he had mistaken Olivia for the ghost of Eliza was nothing but a fantasy and he was wildly adrift, which brought him back again to the sheer size of the sum someone had paid Eliza. Had she threatened to tell Sir Wolford or the Tucketts that Olivia had taken lovers? Was it something to do with the complication of yet another bastard child, this time Eliza's? Was the baby Tuckett's and had she threatened to tell Olivia? But surely that would not have resulted in her death. If his experience of young blades like Tuckett was anything to go by, bastards by servant girls were commonplace. He might offer her five or even ten guineas to go away and say nothing, but never a hundred. He might even find it something to brag about to his friends, especially as there was no sign of a legitimate heir. Nothing Simon could think of seemed to justify such an extreme as murder.

Then there was the clumsy attempt on his life. If it was not at the behest of a member of Sir Wolford's household then who else did his evidence threaten? He wondered if there were likely to be any more attempts. He recalled his boastful remarks to Francis Down at the Inquest, that he could more than handle himself with a sword, and doubted very much if it were still true. His work and the bad weather had meant he had taken little exercise of late and he was greatly out of condition.

Unable to settle to anything satisfactorily, Simon decided to seek out one of his patients who ran a fencing school behind the Green Dragon tavern and see if he were free to give him a few bouts with the rapier.

The hour which followed was an energetic one. The fencing master, realising Simon was somewhat rusty, let him off lightly to begin with but after a brief rest got down to some serious work from which Simon emerged sweating and breathless. 'Not bad,' said his teacher, 'but you really do need more practice.'

Simon agreed. 'But it's difficult to fit it in when I'm as busy as I've been these last months.'

'So what brought you here now?' enquired the fencing

master as he cleaned his own foil before putting it away.

'Because I needed the exercise. And also because last week someone tried to kill me.'

The teacher stopped what he was doing. 'Seriously?'

'Oh very seriously, I can assure you.'

'Presumably it was some opportunist cutpurse, for surely as a doctor you've few enemies?' Simon said nothing. 'You look doubtful. Are you suggesting there was more to it?'

'I suppose it could just have been bad luck and I ran into a common thief but I rather think it had to do with a matter which I've been looking into recently for the attempt was made when I was on my way to give evidence at an Inquest. If that's the case, then it might well be that whoever was behind it tries again.'

'I see,' said the fencing master. 'And did you fight him?'

'It wasn't possible. He came at me from behind in a narrow alley and it would've been impossible to draw my sword even if I'd been wearing it which I wasn't. It was all I could do to grapple with him as you can see.' He held out his hand with its now healing scar.

The man regarded it. 'If you're right then I suggest you practise your swordplay more regularly and that you take your rapier with you wherever you go. I'll also show you, to the best of my ability, how to deal with the assassin who comes up behind with dagger or rope if you think it might be useful. So if you're game we'll try a few throws and falls before you stiffen up completely.'

By the time Simon returned home he was aching in every limb but in spite of this the irritable, restless mood refused to leave him. Finally, telling Anna that he wouldn't be in for supper, he went out again, ate in a tavern, then paid a rare visit to a gaming house where he played at dice until nearly midnight before picking up a friendly whore to whom he'd had recourse before. He then went back to her lodgings with her and, after a suitable interval of sport, slept like a log.

He returned home early the next morning to find Anna in a highly agitated state. Not merely one but two messengers had been round to the house with urgent letters for him. Tossing his cloak and sword into a corner Simon went into the kitchen demanding his breakfast as he sat down and opened them. The first, couched more in the style of a demand than an invitation, was from Sir Thomas Monkton asking him to visit him at the Inns of Court at the first possible opportunity. He then turned his attention to the second and his heart sank as he recognised the seal of the Royal College of Physicians. Their summons gave him no choice at all. He was officially called to appear before a special meeting of the Council that very afternoon at three o'clock to answer a grave and serious charge.

Someone had been busy, very busy. He found it hard to believe that the two demands were unconnected, but how or why the Royal College of Physicians had become involved he was unable to imagine, though he had little doubt they would find an excuse to condemn him if they could if past history was anything to go on. An awful thought struck him. Was it anything to do with the missing poppy syrup?

* * *

It was in a state of acute depression that he set off for his first appointment, that with Sir Thomas Monkton at the Inns of Court. He arrived, sent in his name, and was then left to kick his heels outside his rooms for half an hour or more. When he was finally shown in Monkton wasted no time in coming to the point.

'Ah, Dr Forman. I have here a letter from Sir Wolford Barnes of which I think you should take careful note. In it he writes that his daughter has now told him that the girl Eliza Pargeter had taken a violent lover who had assaulted her on a number of occasions and that in spite of warnings from her mistress that she should dissociate herself from him for her own safety, she had refused to do so. What do you say to that?'

So that was it. 'That I wonder why Lady Olivia Tuckett did not send this information to the Inquest either herself or by Master Down who was also a witness.'

Monkton looked down at the letter again. 'Sir Wolford says that Lady Tuckett was very upset at the girl's death and did not consider it relevant until she heard the verdict, obviously assuming that her maid had drowned herself. Apparently the man's a sailor and must certainly be well away by now if he knows what's good for him. So that most probably is the end of the matter, don't you agree?'

'Possibly. Except that I think it unlikely the girl had a violent lover or indeed had had any lover at all until shortly before her death.'

Monkton gave an exasperated sigh. 'What you think, Dr Forman, is scarcely relevant. The explanation is a good one and I suggest you take the matter no further. You have upset Sir Wolford by involving his household in the way you have and—'

'He could scarcely avoid being involved seeing that the dead girl was his daughter's maid,' broke in Simon.

'Pray don't interrupt me, Dr Forman. I repeat, you have offended and annoyed Sir Wolford who, quite rightly, wants to hear no more of it. He is,' Monkton continued, warming to his theme, 'an extremely powerful man in the City with his reputation to consider. So far as I'm concerned, therefore, this is the end of the matter.'

'Then I'll take my leave,' said Simon. 'I have an appointment with the Royal College of Physicians and have no wish to be late.'

So Sir Wolford had now intervened personally. As Simon trudged off in the direction of Blackfriars on his way to the Physicians' Hall in Knightrider Street he wondered if this new turn of events had been prompted by news of his visit to Stratford St Anne having got back to the merchant, or whether he was acting at his daughter's request. On the whole he was inclined to think not. Olivia Tuckett seemed to him to be the kind of woman who would try to settle things herself. He wondered whether he should find out where Olivia's friend Celia Wynter lived to see if she could confirm that Olivia had indeed spent the evening before Eliza's death with her and, if so, what time she had left. He was well aware that this would be somewhat tricky as he would have to come up with a reason sufficiently believable to avoid being shown the door straight away. He must not raise any suspicions, otherwise his visit would immediately be communicated back to Olivia. Now was not the time.

He approached his meeting with the Physicians' Council with real foreboding. He gave thanks each day for the fact that finally, and with extreme difficulty, he had managed to achieve his ambition to become a fully qualified physician, something almost unheard of for a poor village boy like himself. He was immensely proud of the title 'Doctor', that the great University of Cambridge had recognised his worth and that he had finally achieved a licence from the Royal College.

Through his profession he had acquired real standing in the community, numbering among his patients young lords from Court and wealthy City families, as well as the artisans, players and poor of the Bankside. It would have been easy to set up in practice in a town such as Salisbury, but he had been determined to succeed in London and he had done so triumphantly.

Simon also prided himself on the breadth of his knowledge of the new ideas he had learned in Italy, finding most of his English colleagues conservative to a degree in almost all aspects of medicine and astrology. No doubt it was because of this that he had been accused of necromancy and certainly it had suited some members of the Royal College to encourage the idea. But underneath his confidence in his skill and pleasure at the status he had achieved, there still lurked the ghost of the boy who had spent twelve months in a filthy gaol for crossing the local squire. Had Sir Wolford also complained to the Royal College as well as the coroner?

He arrived at the Physicians' Hall some fifteen minutes later and was immediately taken by a servant who told him he was expected in the great Council Chamber. The servant knocked, opened the door and Simon was ushered in to be confronted by the full Council all in their long gowns and seated down both sides of a long polished table, at the far end of which sat the president. He was motioned to a chair placed at its near end.

'You have been called here yet again, Dr Forman,' said the president, 'to answer a charge of grave misconduct. You may be seated.'

Simon sat down. The president riffled through a number of parchments then began. 'Doctors and Censors of the Royal College of Physicians, I will remind you of Dr Forman's previous transgressions.

'First he was called before us because of his treatise on the writings of the heretical Paracelsus, our College being corporately bound to the orthodoxy of Galen in the field of anatomy. Is that not so, Dr Forman?'

Simon agreed that this was indeed so, adding that the College was now so far behind the times that it had been overtaken by almost the whole of the rest of Europe who now quoted Vesalius on anatomy. 'The closer knowledge of Galen has led to no improvements in the physician's art,' he concluded.

Not surprisingly this provoked a cold response from the president who continued without comment, 'Next, sirs, Dr Forman was called here to explain his method of treating those with the great wasting disease with an electuary of sweet roses in wormwood water and then

127

charting the progress of these patients by the use of astronomical almanacs. Those of you who were present will recall that the great Dr William Gilbert, our then president, examined Dr Forman on the principles of astrology and found him sadly lacking. Thereupon he was fined five guineas.

'On the third occasion, having by now somehow acquired the recognition and support of the University of Cambridge,' sneered the president in tones of the utmost contempt, 'he was again examined, this time on the subject of physic, which he claims to have learned from the obscure Dr Cox, and also once more on astrology. With regard to the latter he was found to be ignorant of what we in this country consider its most common principles. This time the four Censors of the College fined him ten pounds. On that occasion it was also felt he should be committed to prison as a charlatan and possible necromancer, but for reasons unknown to us this was prevented by the direct intervention of Secretary of State to the Privy Council, the late Sir Francis Walsingham himself. You have something to say, Dr Forman?'

There was a buzz of noise around the table as Simon rose to his feet. 'I do not know, gentlemen, why you have sent for me yet again. But at least I would like to put the previous record straight. You have found me guilty on three occasions because many of your methods and beliefs are outdated.' At this there was a positive outcry. 'Hear me out, gentlemen, please, though I realise that you are no doubt impatient to condemn me for some other and unknown misdemeanour. What damned me in your eyes wasn't Galen versus Paracelsus or which method of astrology I use but the fact that we disagree on basic principles of medicine. For instance, I do not hold with continual blood-letting, it merely weakens the patient; nor with judging the progress of all complaints by peering at bottles of paltry piss!'

The president quelled the uproar that followed. 'Dr Forman,' he said in a fury, 'you have hardly helped yourself with regard to this latest complaint.' He picked up a paper which he held up to the assembly. 'Which is that you have meddled in the affairs of others in a manner totally unbefitting a physician. I have here a complaint from Sir Wolford Barnes, the eminent merchant venturer, in which he states that having first alleged that his daughter's maid was foully murdered, you took it upon yourself to go into the country and trespass on his estate, gossip in the local tavern and then compound your behaviour further by closely interrogating one of his servants with regard to the girl's death. We await your explanation.'

So that was it. Sir Wolford certainly had been busy. It was unlikely that he had come up with this himself, thought Simon. Once again he did not think it the work of Olivia Tuckett and certainly not that of her unintelligent husband. The most likely instigator therefore had to be Francis Down.

'We're waiting, Dr Forman,' said the president.

'No doubt I'm damned before I open my mouth,' said Simon. 'So I'll be as brief as possible. Totally fortuitously the dead girl was brought to my house having been found dead in the river, whereupon I recognised her as a patient who had consulted me some four months previously. An examination proved beyond doubt that she was with child and also, to my own satisfaction, that she had been bound before drowning. This I told the Inquest, and the jury, I gather against the coroner's wishes, brought in a verdict of wilful murder. Some days later I was in the village of Stratford St Anne where I put up overnight having business the next day in Ipswich. Again fortuitously,' he lied, 'I discovered the same girl was to be buried in the village the following day. In passing I would say it was my servant, not I, who gossiped in the tavern. As you might imagine such a tragedy was the subject of much discussion. I had gone to bed.

'The girl's burial took place as we were about to leave the next morning and the clergyman, Dr James Field, hearing that I was in the village and a doctor, sent for me and asked me a number of questions regarding the symptoms of drowning, which I answered to the best of my ability. He had thought it likely the girl took her own life and was therefore doubtful about her right to a churchyard burial. From him I learned where the poor girl's parents lived and visited them briefly to express my condolences. I do not consider that constitutes trespassing on Sir Wolford Barnes's estate. That's all, gentlemen. Why it should be a matter of serious complaint, I am at a loss to understand.'

The president could hardly contain himself. 'Do you not see, Dr Forman, that *none* of this was your business? You did not have to examine the girl. It was unlikely you would have been called to give evidence at the Inquest had you not offered to do so. And even if your visit to Stratford St Anne was as you describe "fortuitous",' he continued contemptuously, 'you had played your part in the affair and it was no longer any business of yours. But I say to you frankly, I do not believe you were in Essex by chance, but had gone there, as Sir Wolford asserts, to meddle in his affairs.' There was a general murmur of agreement at this.

'Cast the fellow out,' called out an old greybeard to general applause. 'It would seem he learned his skills under a hedge!' Another muttered that he had no truck with so-called physicians who had spent time learning heathenish practices in foreign parts.

'We agree, gentlemen, therefore, that this time we should withdraw Dr Forman's licence to practise?' asked the president. 'Will you show this in the usual manner?

'Thank you, gentlemen. You have gone too far, Forman, and on behalf of the Council and Censors of the Royal College of Physicians I pronounce that your licence to practise is hereby revoked. This time you can hardly appeal to those in high places. Sir Francis Walsingham is dead and whatever means you used to have him intervene for you before, you are unlikely to be able to persuade his successor, Sir Robert Cecil, to interest himself in your affairs. His views on heresy and necromancy are well known.'

'And equally well known is the fact that his position has yet to be ratified by the Queen,' replied Simon, shaking with anger.

The president was icy. 'You do understand what this means?'

'Most certainly. But I'd also remind you that your writ runs only within the City. I choose to live on the Bankside where my Cambridge qualification is sufficient, though I cannot pretend that this unwarranted punishment is not extremely damaging. But I can assure you all, I'll not rest until you are forced to restore my licence to me again.'

'Idle threats, Dr Forman, idle threats,' replied the president. 'Leave us. We have nothing more to say to you.'

Simon walked down the steps and out into a watery sunshine sick at heart. He wondered what on earth was in store for him next. For the first time he wished to God that Eliza had been hauled out of the river anywhere else along the Thames but the Bankside.

Chapter 10

Tides on the Thames

Marcus Tuckett returned from Kent some days later in a state of gloom laced with irritation. The seizure had left Lord Tuckett with slurred speech and without movement in his left side which meant, according to his father's doctor, that he might live for months or could suffer a second and fatal attack at any time. Therefore he must be prepared to go down to Kent to be with him for a considerable period of time if it became necessary.

'Father's even now making his final Will with his lawyer,' he told Olivia. 'And still with no sign of a grandson – unless you've conceived in this last month.'

'If I haven't it's scarcely my fault,' she retorted.

'Well it certainly isn't mine,' Marcus replied in his usual sulky manner. 'I'm beginning to wonder if I haven't married into barren stock. I'll tell you now,' he boasted, 'that there are two girls in Kent who've already borne me bastards, indeed one child's still at the breast. Therefore the failure, Olivia, would seem to lie with you.'

'We are but four months married,' she said with some heat, 'and these are early days. But since you are so concerned, you must know that I've consulted a physician who is said to have skill in these matters.' Originally she had intended to tell him that it was Simon Forman as Marcus had appeared to find the doctor amusing but in view of her father's actions she could not possibly do so now. Neither he nor Francis Down had been able to contain themselves with pleasure when letters in answer to Sir Wolford's had arrived from both Sir Thomas Monkton and the president of the Royal College of Physicians. Sir Thomas wrote that he had summoned Dr Forman and made it clear to him that in the light of new evidence he considered the case was now closed, while the president of the Royal College informed the merchant in formal terms that Dr Simon Forman's licence to practise medicine in the City of London had been revoked.

'And what did this doctor say to you?' asked Marcus.

'He told me I was foolish to be anxious so soon for while some brides conceive on their wedding night, many do not and may not succeed for weeks or even months.'

'One of my girls in Kent gave me a child after but one night's tumbling,' he replied sourly. 'And I certainly did my utmost on our wedding night as well as after it.' He looked her over from head to toe. 'I'll tell you now that before we were betrothed I heard many rumours about your virtue – or lack of it. But the size of your dowry and the marriage settlement were sufficient for my father to order me to quell any doubts I might have and in the event it appears they were unfounded. But this doesn't alter the position now. My father expected news of an heir before his death.'

'Then let us hope we can provide it,' replied Olivia and walked away, forbearing to point out that even if she did have a child there was no guarantee it would be a son.

The weather had improved considerably during the last two days and so she took herself off to the garden behind the house. There were few flowers yet in bloom but there was a pleasant perfume from the creeping thyme on the path and the sage bushes in the herb patch. She wiped a wooden bench with her kerchief and sat down, her mind in turmoil. For much of her life she had proved adept at manipulating events to her advantage but now she felt she was being carried along on a tide of events she was unable to control.

Her birth had been a sad disappointment to her father, not only because he had wanted a son but because her mother was content from then on to retire into the life of a semi-invalid leaving Olivia to be brought up in the country largely by nursemaids. Fortunately at about the time Sir Wolford finally faced up to the fact that Olivia would be his only child he also recognised that she was unusual in that she was both pretty and clever. After some years of living in Shoemakers Row he had bought the large house close to Bishopsgate and he now took her back to London with him, employing a sensible woman to act as a chaperone. He also engaged a tutor to give her some basic learning but she proved so apt a pupil that she soon outgrew him.

From a new teacher she discovered she had a flair for languages which Sir Wolford realised could be put to good use as he didn't speak or understand anything except his native English. A daughter who could speak both French and Italian was therefore a considerable asset to him when

European merchants visited him at his house. As she grew older she became invaluable in other ways, for Lady Barnes rarely left Stratford St Anne, leaving him in need of a hostess when he entertained.

The way of life suited both father and daughter until she was into her mid-teens. Sir Wolford was now indulgent and nothing was too good for his prize possession, from a closet full of fine gowns to a thoroughbred horse for when she chose to ride. It was hardly surprising therefore that by the time she was sixteen suitors for her hand were knocking on Sir Wolford's door but for the time being both were content to let matters rest. It was then Olivia discovered a far more pleasurable activity than any she had tried before; and for that, also, she showed considerable aptitude.

But the pleasant pattern of life was soon rudely interrupted. So long as she was accompanied by a maid or servant she had a good deal of licence to go where she chose. She particularly enjoyed visiting the playhouses, the Theatre and the Curtain, near Finsbury Field, and the new Rose playhouse on the Bankside, and she was soon familiar with the latest plays and the players who acted in them. So it was she met Charles Sheldon, a dark and charismatic young actor who was just beginning to make a name for himself. Liaisons between actors and their admirers in the audience were by no means uncommon but the women involved were almost always married, the affair undertaken without commitment on either side and with the utmost discretion.

But Olivia, while she might have been a bright student

in many ways, was inexperienced in others and so fell passionately in love with Charles. The affair soon progressed beyond sighs, bad verse and handholding to matters more robust. Sir Wolford's absence for some weeks in Essex gave the young couple the opportunity they needed and they took to bed whenever and wherever they could, heedless of the proprieties. Looking back on it now Olivia realised just how foolish and careless she had been, for no sooner had her father returned to London than some neighbours took it on themselves to inform him that he'd best look to his daughter's conduct if he didn't want to be left with damaged goods and a possible bastard.

A stormy and tearful scene followed, resulting in Olivia being sent at once to her mother in Essex for six months and when she did finally return to London it was a long time before she was allowed out of the house unless accompanied by her father or someone he could trust to see she behaved herself. As to Charles Sheldon, shortly after all communication between the two of them had ceased, he was set on one night after leaving the theatre and thrashed until he could hardly stand. Her father never referred to the subject again but Olivia knew only too well who must have instigated the attack.

Two years later, bored and stifled by her situation, she had embarked on an affair with Francis Down, which brought her to a pretty pass.

Simon lay sleepless and staring at the ceiling all night after his confrontation with the Royal College. His words might have been brave but they were, as was pointed out to him, only words. The future looked bleak. It seemed as if everything for which he had striven for so long was to come to nothing. He was not even sure exactly what the revoking of his licence would mean. The area of the Bankside lay outside the jurisdiction of the City of London in the See of the Bishop of Winchester which is why the playhouses, gaming dens and brothels flourished there and the whores were known as Winchester geese. But did it really apply to the practice of medicine?

Of course he could go into the country and once fifty miles or even less from London set up in practice claiming he was a member of the Royal College and it would be unlikely anyone would dispute it but he had been determined from the first that he must be successful in the capital. The immediate problems were practical. Should he try to continue practising in the city although he had many patients south of the river, most of whom were poor and could afford to pay him little or nothing? The main source of his income lay on the north side in Middlesex and the City. The handful of the better off in Southwark such as Philip Henslowe (who rarely dosed himself with his own medicines) and his actor son-in-law, Ned Alleyn, could not possibly make up for the loss of the City merchants and their families or the wealthy householders who were moving into the now fashionable Blackfriars. If Simon risked trying to treat them regardless then it was certain the Physicians would have him in gaol, and Queen Elizabeth's great Spymaster was no longer there to defend him as he had before.

Simon had always refused to seek out a rich and influential patron as many physicians did, not wishing to be at the beck and call of some person for whom he might well have little liking or respect. But had he been under such patronage it would have been more difficult for the Royal College to have acted in the way they had and he now wondered if his attitude had not been one of arrogant folly. Unless he found some way to force the College to alter its decision, he was staring financial ruin in the face.

Even if he humiliated himself by crawling to Sir Wolford and swearing on oath he would never interfere in his affairs again he doubted it would make the slightest difference; the merchant was obviously determined to make an example of him. That left him with only one course of action. To discover – and quickly – exactly how Eliza had met her death and what had led up to it, in the hope that he might use the information to force Sir Wolford to make the Royal College give him his licence back or risk the disclosure of a major scandal. That is if he could manage to stay alive to do it! For Simon was now certain that Eliza's murder lay either at the door of the merchant or a member of his household.

What he needed desperately was more information. It was obviously out of the question for him to go anywhere near Bishopsgate himself and so he sent for John Bradedge and briefly explained the desperate situation to him.

'Here's your chance to make some restitution for your carelessness,' Simon concluded, 'and also to give me some prospect of being able to keep you both on. If I remember rightly there's a row of smaller houses opposite to that of Sir Wolford. Houses, presumably, of respectable artisans and their families. I want you to go there in the guise of an honest workman, knock on doors and ask those within if they have any tasks you might do to earn a few honest pence. You can say truthfully that you were in the wars in the Low Countries. Give them chapter and verse if they ask.'

'What kind of tasks?' asked John, sounding doubtful. 'I can't turn my hand to anything and everything I might be asked to do.'

'Then if you're asked to do something you can't you'll have to say so, but you're a practical fellow and shouldn't find it too difficult. Wear your oldest and shabbiest breeches, put a leather jerkin over your shirt, a sacking apron round your waist and take a bag of tools with you and a saddler's needle and thread. What you really need to find is one of those women who have little else to occupy them but spying on their neighbours. You know the sort I mean. They hover with the door ajar listening to what's being said outside in the street, or lurk behind the casement to see what the neighbours are getting up to. What I want to know is if there was any unusual activity in or around Sir Wolford's house the night before Eliza's body was found, strangers hanging around, late night comings and goings, anything untoward.'

He yawned and stretched his arms for he had had little sleep. 'In the meantime I'm going to try and find the wherryman who hauled Eliza out of the river to see if he's able to give me any idea where she might have gone in, but it'll take some time for I can't for the life of me remember his name and there must be hundreds of wherrymen.'

'I'll be off then,' said John, 'but if I remember rightly, didn't the wherryman say you'd lanced an abscess for him back last year sometime?'

John's suggestion proved useful. As soon as his servant had left, Simon applied himself to going carefully back through his Casebook, eventually discovering what he hoped was the correct entry: '4th August 1590. Lancing an abscess on the neck of one Will Hudson, wherryman. For the lancing 6d, for salve of white wax mixed with powdered camphor and four drops of almond oil 4d. Wound cleaned of pus.'

Armed with this knowledge he immediately went to look for Hudson. For what seemed an age his search was fruitless. He tried all the taverns used by watermen of all kinds, walked from one set of watersteps to the next asking the jostling wherrymen at their foot if anyone knew where he might find his man but to no avail. All he could do was leave a message at every set of steps to the effect that Dr Forman wanted to see Will Hudson urgently and if he would come to his house he would make it worth his while.

He was almost home when a chorus of shouts from the river brought him to a halt. He looked down into the water to see Hudson pulling away from a group of his colleagues.

'I hear you want to speak to me, Dr Forman,' he shouted. 'I've a fare here to go to Blackfriars. I'll be with you in half an hour.'

He was as good as his word. Simon let him in and he glanced askance at the open study door, no doubt with memories of what he had undergone in there the previous year, but Simon took him through to the kitchen and asked Anna to give the wherryman some ale. Hudson sat down obviously uneasy at what might come next.

Simon came up behind him and peered at his neck. 'The wound seems to have healed all right.'

'Clean as a whistle, Doctor. Oh, and I must also thank you for taking that corpse off my hands and going to the 'quest. I'd lost half a morning as it was.'

'It's about that girl I want to talk to you.'

The wherryman shook his head. 'It seems it's a funny business from what I've heard. They say there's more to it than a silly lovesick maid drowning herself over some man, but that someone put her there.'

'I think someone did.' Simon pushed across to Hudson a roughly drawn map showing the course of the Thames from Kew to Deptford. 'What I'd like to know from you is where it might have happened. If it helps I think she'd been dead only a few hours when you hauled her out.'

'Where did she live?' asked Hudson.

'In the City. Near to Bishopsgate.'

Hudson sucked his teeth and screwed up his face. 'Well she certainly didn't go in anywhere near there for we found her not so far downriver from Westminster and anyway if I was going to do a job like that I'd get well out of town. There's a deal too much going on both sides of the river here, and even with this poor summer it's still light till late on. So let's say whoever it was took her out into the country. I'd settle for Chelsea. It's quiet up there.

'Let's see. When I picked up my passenger over from the Wandsworth fields, the tide was going out fast, helped by the rain which had fallen upriver. I reckon she must have been taken out in a boat and dumped midstream otherwise she'd have just floated back to the shore. Now it's only a guess but seeing where she was when we found her, I'd say it was very probable she went in somewhere along Chelsea Reach. I might be quite wrong, of course.'

'Go on, you're doing fine,' said Simon.

'Well, we boatmen reckon on average between those two points the ebb tide lasts for seven hours and the flood for five. It alters a bit of course if there's a lot of water coming downriver or a strong tide flowing up with a following wind but that's about right. So, if they threw her in midstream about eleven o'clock or even a bit later, the flow would be coming in fast but being City folk they'd not think about the state of the tide. So first she'd be carried upriver for a bit, maybe even get caught up on something – the river twists a lot up there – until dead water. Then, when the tide turned and flowed out so strongly, she'd come down with it. Mind,' Hudson added, 'I'm only saying what might have happened. It could all have been different.'

'Maybe, but it makes sense,' said Simon. 'You've helped me a great deal. Have another drink and here's a crown for your trouble, Will. One more thing; I'd rather you didn't tell anyone about our discussion, but keep your eyes and ears open. You watermen know most of what passes on the Thames. If you think there's anything I should know, come back. There'll be another crown for you.'

Hudson pocketed the coin and took up the tankard, sinking half its contents in one swallow. Then, looking suddenly grave, he asked, 'Do you reckon the poor maid was already dead when she went into the water, Doctor?'

Simon sighed and shrugged his shoulders. 'I don't know. I hope for her sake that she was but I think it more likely she was heavily drugged. That being the case it's not possible to tell if she came round when the cold water closed over her head. If she did it must have been a terrifying death.'

'Well, Doctor,' said Hudson, finishing his drink and putting the tankard down with a thump, 'if what you say's true I'll reserve an early place at Tyburn to see the bastard hanged that did it.'

Shortly after noon Simon rode over the bridge en route for Chelsea. He made his way through Blackfriars then along the Strand to Westminster, passing close to the great Palace and the mighty Abbey. Like the City, Westminster too was growing, but he soon found himself riding between gardens and orchards towards open fields. The countryside here was foreign to him for he had little time since coming to London to explore outside the immediate area of his work. His route took him near enough to the river to catch glimpses of it sparkling in the rare sunshine. The scene was a tranquil one. Men worked in the fields and in house and cottage gardens, women were making the most of the weather to hang linen over the bushes to dry.

Finally Simon came to a crossroads where a well-used lane led down towards the water. Tethering his horse to a convenient tree, he set out to explore his immediate surroundings and after walking for only a few minutes he found himself at the head of a short creek. It was half tide revealing extensive mud banks along both sides. At least the mud flats here were clean and did not stink like those nearer home where rivers like the Fleet, little better than sewers, flowed into the Thames. It was very quiet and there was no one about. The nearest property, a substantial farmhouse with two large barns, was about a quarter of a mile away. It was a good place if you didn't want to be seen.

Moreover, there were several small boats hauled up on to the mud and secured to old posts, their oars tucked neatly inside them. It would obviously be easy to unhitch and use one of them. Two or three vacant posts with rings attached suggested their owners were currently elsewhere.

It was a warm day and Simon sat down on a tree stump trying to imagine, if this was the place, how Eliza had been brought here. Was she drugged and bound and brought in a carriage? That seemed too risky even if the place was remote. Or had she been lured to the spot by some means, but if so, how had she then been persuaded to drink the poppy syrup?

From the river came the sound of oars and soon a boat appeared rowed by a sturdy-looking middle-aged man. He guided it into the side of the creek, jumped out, sinking half-way up his boots in the mud, then hauled the boat up behind him and secured it to one of the empty posts. At this point the sound of whistling could be heard from behind Simon and he looked round to see a boy of about twelve walking briskly down the path, a fishing rod over his shoulder.

The sight apparently enraged the boatman. 'You imp of Satan!' he shouted. 'You Devil's cub!'

The boy stopped in his tracks. 'What are you bawling at me like that for, Master George?'

'You've had my boat again, haven't you, you slubber-degullion! No doubt you were sneaking down here even now to do it again, thinking I wouldn't find out.'

The boy looked aggrieved. 'But I haven't, Master George. Honestly. Not since you clapped me round the ears for doing it two months since. Not that I did it any harm,' he muttered to himself. Seeing he had made little impression the boy continued, 'And I wasn't coming to take it now either. I'm going along the path upriver to see if I can catch something as the tide comes in.'

'Well someone had my boat last week,' said the boatman in a tone of disbelief. 'And if it wasn't you, who was it?'

'How should I know? Are you sure someone did? You could be wrong.'

'I know someone took it because it wasn't tied up on my post where I left it, that's why. It was put on Jess Walker's post and he's been complaining about it ever since.'

'If it had been me,' said the boy, 'then I'd have had more wit than to do that.'

Master George looked unconvinced. Looking round he spied Simon on his tree trunk and included him in the conversation. 'Time was,' he said, 'when you could leave your boat here without any worry.'

'I thought you must be honest in these parts,' replied Simon, 'when I saw the oars left in the boats. No one would dare do that where I live.'

'Where are you from then?' asked the boatman.

'I live in Southwark,' Simon replied. 'I came out here for a breath of fresh air.'

'Can I go now?' asked the lad.

Master George sighed. 'Oh, very well. But if I catch you taking my boat again I'll take a stick to you. When I was a lad we showed some respect to our neighbours and their goods. Nowadays you're allowed to do as you like.'

'But I didn't take your boat,' the boy reiterated. 'I don't care if you believe me or not, but I *didn't*!' He sloped off along a path running beside the river and disappeared out of sight.

The boatman spat. 'Young varmint!' Then, in answer to Simon's enquiry as to what had happened to the boat, he replied, 'Last Tuesday's a week my neighbour Jess comes roaring round banging on the door at six in the morning to say my boat's on his post. They're fussy about that kind of thing round here. It's only a few weeks since I caught that young villain rowing it back in bold as brass when by rights he should have been working in his dad's fields. So it seems likely to me that he'd done it again.'

Simon made suitably sympathetic noises. 'Time was,' continued his companion, 'when there were so many boats and it was so busy here that he wouldn't have dared do it as someone would have seen him. But the creek's got that silted up that many folk now keep their boats higher upriver. It's even worse this year with all the mud brought down by the rain.'

Simon agreed the weather had been foul, then asked where he might find an inn for refreshment, explaining where he'd left his horse. The boatman said the Six Bells was nearby and he'd put him on his road as he was going that way himself. They walked up the lane to the cross-roads in companionable silence. As they reached the higher ground Simon looked across to the farm with its barns.

'That's a tidy place,' he said. 'The land here must make a farmer a warm man from the look of those two fine barns.'

'John Kenton, you mean?' said the boatman. 'I reckon he does well enough but it's not his land. He's the tenant. An ordinary farming man like him'd never be able to afford to have a place like that.'

Quite suddenly Simon had a premonition of what was to come next.

'Oh no,' continued his informant. 'The farm and land used to belong to a family called Field in Essex. It came to them by way of a settlement when one of them married an heiress from round here years back. Now it belongs to some wealthy merchant in the City.'

Chapter 11

The Watcher at the Window

Simon had not been the only one to lie sleepless and apprehensive, his thoughts circling round and round in his head. Olivia had done likewise as again and again she went over the disastrous result of the plan. At first she had refused to believe Eliza: 'You must be mistaken. You are, after all, inexperienced in these matters.'

Eliza was adamant. 'No, mistress. I've not seen my courses these two months, besides which I feel sickly of a morning and have a soreness in the breasts of which I've heard other women speak.'

Olivia remained unconvinced. 'But how could it be so after only the one time?'

'Dr Forman told me that once can be enough!'

'You've actually consulted him about this?' asked Olivia with rising alarm.

'No, no, mistress,' Eliza reassured her. 'Not since I first went to the doctor for my horoscope and your sleeping draught. I asked him then if a girl could conceive the first time she was bedded. He said she could. He seemed to find it amusing, thinking I'd a lover who was trying to talk me into lying with him by persuading me there was no risk. But,' she continued with a sigh, 'I found it hard to believe him and so said nothing to you. And now what am I to do?'

'Return to your parents and that soon,' replied Olivia immediately. 'They must find you a husband. The money I gave you will amply provide a dowry.'

'They money you gave me, mistress, was for a bargain. And that bargain I kept. There was no mention made of any child. Now I am trapped and you tell me all I have to do is go quietly away and find some clod to marry me. Why should I have to spoil my life in this way?'

'Then you must go to the woman who attended on me and ask her to rid you of it.'

Eliza shook her head. 'And risk death as you did, mistress? I think not. No, if I'm to bear this child I think it only right you give me a further sum.'

Olivia looked aghast. 'You can't possibly mean that! God's blood, girl, a hundred guineas is a dowry for a squire's daughter.'

'I have already divided the sum up between members of my family. The child I'm carrying must be decently brought up. If it's a boy then it should be properly educated, if a girl then she will need a decent dowry. If, as you say, I must find a man who will act father to it, then surely – let's say – a further fifty guineas – is reasonable? For now.'

The implication behind the last words was not lost on Olivia. 'For now? What do you mean "for now"?'

'There will be expenses for my lying-in, childbed linen and good clothing for the baby, possibly even a wet nurse should I prove unable to suckle it. But fifty guineas is hardly likely to cover the cost of my bringing it up.'

Olivia stared at her in horror. 'Providing you with the first sum was hard enough. How in the name of all that's holy am I to find another so soon? It's impossible.'

'Then,' replied Eliza quietly, 'I see no alternative but to do my duty and tell Sir Marcus the truth. After all, every-thing is changed now.'

Olivia clenched her hands until the knuckles were white. 'He'll never believe you!'

The girl smiled her catlike smile. 'Shall we put it to the test then, mistress?'

Olivia had found herself turning to Francis Down. And he too demanded a price.

Simon rode back from Chelsea deep in thought. There was no way of proving, of course, that his informant's boat had been taken for any purpose more serious than an unauthorised night's fishing, but added to the fact that Sir Wolford owned land nearby, it made its use for a more sinister purpose a very real possibility. He resolved to question Olivia's alibi as soon as he could. He took his time riding home and it was early evening by the time he reached it.

John Bradedge was there before him and it was clear he had much to report. He greeted his master with a stream of disconnected information involving mean gossips, noises in the street and late night assignations.

Simon pleaded with him to calm down and begin at the beginning. 'Let's go through everything in order. That way we can see what's important and what isn't.'

It could not be said that John had enjoyed his day. Half the householders sent him about his business and while some had been reasonably polite, others had felt impelled to remind him of the laws governing the conduct of 'rogues, vagabonds and sturdy beggars'. Those who did condescend to employ him gave him only the most unpleasant tasks to carry out, as a result of which he had found himself moving a midden to the end of the street for a man who'd been fined for keeping it outside his front door, stitching up the sides of a pair of smelly boots for another (a time-consuming task for which he'd been ill rewarded) and sweeping out a stable for a third, and all without making any progress whatsoever towards the real purpose of his mission.

His enquiries as to 'who lives at the big house over the road?' had been met all too often with a suspicious look and 'what do you want to know for?', the inference being that he required the information for some felonious purpose such as burglary. By the end of the afternoon he was convinced he was on a fool's errand. Until, that is, he knocked on the door of Enid Fitzwarren.

She was an unprepossessing woman of uncertain years with a lantern jaw, her face set in a permanent expression of dismal annoyance. Unlike most busy housewives she was impeccably dressed as if for a formal visit, her stiff dark gown with its spotless wide collar proclaiming that she favoured the Puritan tendency, while her house was so spectacularly tidy it looked unlived in. Enid told John that she'd just taken delivery of half a cartload of logs and he could stack them neatly for her in the yard at the back of the house if he wanted to make himself useful.

She stood over him all the while as he did so giving him the benefit of a constant diatribe of complaint against all her neighbours. John had found exactly the sort of person Simon had described, for Enid's days indeed passed eavesdropping on all around her. It seemed the whole world had set themselves against her. The neighbours were noisy and spiteful, the children unruly. The men were idle good-for-nothings whose only thought was to chase the wenches and get drunk in the taverns, while the women couldn't wait for their husbands to leave home for work before they let their lovers in by the back door. She alone was respectable, decent, a good neighbour and an upright citizen who knew her duty. He'd be shocked, therefore, to learn what people had to say about her, a statement which led John to mutter under his breath that he doubted it. Her own husband was, apparently, a paragon of virtue applying himself industriously to his craft of bookbinding from early morning till late, very late, at night.

When he could finally get a word in edgeways (for Enid offered him no refreshment) he wondered who lived in the big house across the street. An obsequious smile spread across her face. That was the house of Sir Wolford Barnes, the great merchant venturer. A very rich and powerful man but not too grand to greet Enid and her husband if he met them in the street, unlike some. Her expression sharpened, however, when she came to the rest of the household. The daughter had behaved more like a trollop from St Paul's Yard than a great man's daughter – she could tell him a thing or two about what had gone on, indeed she could. Her voice sank to a whisper. 'They say she disgraced herself with one of the players from the Curtain Theatre when she was but sixteen years old!'

Now the young madam was married (and not a moment too soon) but her husband was little better than a wastrel, even if he was the son of a lord, rolling in at all hours of the night roaring drunk and banging on the gate to wake the porter and so keeping honest Godfearing folk from their sleep.

In fact these days it seemed people never stopped going in and out of the house at all hours of the day and night. It was like living in the middle of a marketplace. The previous week had been a case in point. Early one morning there'd been a great to-do as Sir Wolford left in his carriage and she'd happened to hear him telling a servant he'd be staying overnight with a fellow merchant near Barnes. A short while later his son-in-law had ridden away in great haste, accompanied by his groom.

As if that wasn't enough activity for one day, a couple of hours later her ladyship had also clattered off on her horse in the company of that sly-looking secretary of theirs, 'the one who looks at you as if you're the dirt in the kennel'.

Enid had retired to bed early that night as should all respectable folk but the disturbance to the peace of the neighbourhood hadn't ended there. It seemed she'd scarcely shut her eyes before she was woken. 'And do you know what I saw?' she asked John triumphantly, as he laboured over the growing stack of logs.

John said he couldn't imagine.

'It was that secretary again. I must have missed seeing him and her ladyship coming back. Anyway there he was with that white-haired wench who was the lady's maid—' She stopped. 'It's said she's dead, pulled out of the river. I say let it be a lesson to all light wenches who are without shame. My mother brought *me* up to be clean-living, Godfearing and know my place. And no man would have laid a finger on me before he'd taken me to the altar.'

John said he could well believe it but, afraid she would now launch off into another sermon on fornication and adultery without giving him any more information, he quickly reminded her that she had just started to tell him that she had seen this loose young woman in the street with a male servant late at night.

So Enid resumed her tale. 'It must have been all of ten o'clock when I heard the sound of a horse outside. Well, naturally, I got up and looked out from behind the curtain.'

'Naturally,' responded John.

'Well, there they were and even though it was dark, there being no moon, I could see he had his arm round her shoulders, talking to her, though I couldn't hear what they were saying. Then he mounts the horse and up she gets behind him on the pillion and off they go down the street. *She* was carrying some kind of travelling bag with her. That speaks for itself. A decent girl wouldn't be going off with a young fellow at that time of night except for one purpose. You mark my words, she let him have his way, encouraged him most likely then, after he'd had his pleasure, off he went leaving her ruined. At least she'd enough decency left to drown herself,' Enid concluded looking thoroughly satisfied at the outcome of her tale.

She had finally left John to finish stacking her wood for which she had reluctantly given him the princely sum of fourpence.

'It seems we've both been in luck,' said Simon, and told John that Will Hudson had surmised about the most likely place Eliza had been put in the water and what he had discovered for himself at Chelsea Creek.

'Certainly someone took a boat out either late that Monday night or in the very early hours of Tuesday morning, and Sir Wolford does own land out that way. It seems too much of a coincidence. And now you tell me of this busy harridan who saw Eliza leaving with Down late that evening.'

'She wasn't absolutely sure which day it was when I pressed her,' said John, 'and I didn't like to make too much of it as I thought she might become suspicious.'

'Well, since it was a sufficiently unusual event to cause comment and for her to remember it, let's assume that it was the night Eliza died and she was going off somewhere with Down. Your woman said nothing of any kind of constraint then?'

'On the contrary she assumed the worst and that the two were creeping off somewhere for a quick tumble.'

'And she also said she did not notice Lady Tuckett return?'

'That's right. Which is why she was surprised to see

Down again as she hadn't seen either of them come back although they must have done. Even such an interfering busybody as that couldn't spend all of her time at her window.'

'I wonder.' Simon looked thoughtful. 'Perhaps she didn't, and only he returned. But why? And where was she?'

John was growing tired of all this conjecture. 'Don't you see, Doctor, there you have it. It's like I said at the very beginning of all this. It's all to do with Eliza being with child. She and this Down fellow must have been playing at bedsport, she found she was to have a child and told him he'd best do something about it and that pretty quick. He didn't want to marry her nor risk losing his position if she made trouble for him, so he took her off with him on some pretext or another and drowned her. I suppose he thought that if she was found it would be upriver and no one would ever know what happened to her.'

Simon shook his head. 'I can't believe that's all there is to it. Why should he take such a drastic course? If it was his child and she came to him as you say then she would also come to him as a girl with a dowry of a hundred guineas. I can't imagine marriage to Eliza would be any man's bed of roses but I doubt very much that Down would turn his back on such an offer, especially if pressure was put on him by Sir Wolford and Lady Tuckett and his remaining in their good favour depended on it. And after they'd wed, there's no reason why he shouldn't continue in his post and she in hers, at least for some time. Lady

Tuckett might even have agreed to take her back after the child was born. Such marriages between servants are commonplace. No, I simply don't see it as sufficient motive for murder.'

Chapter 12

Letter to a Lady

Since the next morning brought Simon a number of patients he felt he had no option but to risk treating them regardless, whether or not the jurisdiction of the Royal College included the Bankside. It proved a lengthy business for as well as the usual run of minor ailments and injuries there was a middle-aged woman suffering from increasing pain in her gut whom he had seen before and although he had temporarily been able to relieve the symptoms, it was clear that she was getting steadily weaker.

She wanted him therefore to cast a horoscope to determine the course of the disease if not its cause, and this he had done. The prognosis was not good. Once again he gave her medicine and tried to be comforting but it was obvious to both of them that he was unable to cure her.

After she left he sat awhile in thought aware as always of how, in spite of their skills, there was often so little a physician could do. It was depressing enough when it was a relatively unknown man or woman to whom he had to impart such news. When it was someone much closer then, as he knew from bitter experience, it was devastating.

But in spite of this he had to smile when he saw the

last person waiting to see him. Robert Greene, poet, was one of the most colourful characters on the Bankside. The son of a Norfolk squire, Robin – as he was known to his friends – was able to sign himself 'gentleman' even if his behaviour scarcely warranted it. He claimed to have been to the universities of both Oxford and Cambridge, had finished his education in Europe and was now an established and popular dramatist and the mainstay of the taverns, gaming houses and brothels of the Winchester See. He was complaining, yet again, of having contracted the clap.

Simon briskly examined the offending member. 'Well you know what you must do to avoid it, Robin.'

Greene made an expansive gesture. 'A man must have his sport.'

Simon went over to his shelf and selected his medicines. 'First, here's a salve of Cyprus turpentine. Apply that – regularly!' He then put various seeds into a mortar and ground them up with a wooden pestle.

'And what's that disgusting mess you're making there?' enquired his patient.

'The same as I've given you before. Seeds of anis, coriander and caraway to be mixed with water in which liquorice and sarsaparilla have been boiled. Take it three times a day and if the condition's no better by next week, come back.'

Greene took the bottle and the jar and fumbled in his pocket without success. 'Don't seem to have any money on me,' he informed Simon.

'You *never* have any money on you, Robin.'

'It's the taverns and the gaming houses that are to blame,' said Green shamelessly.

'Then next time ask the tavernkeepers or the owners of the gaming houses to cure you of the clap!' Simon riposted.

Greene assumed an attitude of offended dignity. 'You can afford it, Simon, with all those rich City patients. *I'm* a poet. You should count treating me an honour.'

'It's likely to be an honour I shall soon have to forgo then,' said Simon but refused to explain why. He watched Greene roll off into the alleys of the Bankside no doubt making for the nearest tavern. The poet's behaviour was outrageous but what he had told him was only too true.

There was only one thing for it. Simon would now have to force the issue. It was clear from what John Bradedge had elicited from the dreadful Enid that on the last night before she died Eliza had ridden off somewhere with Francis Down, after which she had never been seen alive again. It was also true, if the wherryman's information on the tides was accurate (which he was sure it was), that she had been put into the river out Chelsea way and that unless he was jumping completely to the wrong conclusion he had discovered not only a suitable place but that a boat had been taken from thence by some unknown person that same night and, even more to the point, that Sir Wolford owned land close to Chelsea Creek.

Simon therefore sat down and wrote a careful letter, addressed to the Lady Olivia Tuckett, in which he told her that he needed to meet her urgently and alone to discuss certain information which had come into his possession regarding the death of her maid. The problem then was how to see it reached her hands only and that no one else saw it. He did not want to send John Bradedge again in case someone, not least the watchful Enid, might recognise him and pass the information on. Nor did he feel he could well involve Anna, not only because her Dutch accent would mark her out but because Olivia had seen her when she visited the house and might well point this out to her husband or father.

It was then his recent session with Robert Greene gave him an idea. Although Greene was a married man, he had left his wife and child behind in Norfolk once he had run through her dowry and, for a long time, had been living with his mistress, Emma Ball. Emma was quite unlike most of the Bankside whores. She and her brother, now a noted highwayman known as 'Cutting Ball Jack', had run wild on the streets since they were children, he keeping them both fed by thieving, she, once she had reached the age of twelve, by whoring.

But by the time she was twenty she was mistress to the great clown, Tarleton, who, much to the disgust of his family, had died in her arms after a session of lovemaking. She had made him happy and had felt genuine affection for him and was much moved to discover that in his Will he had left her a small house. Although his enraged widow had tried her best to have his bequest overruled she had not succeeded. A roof over her head, albeit a small one, gave Emma a certain amount of independence enabling her to choose her customers with rather more care than most. It was still the only occupation open to her apart from lowly service, and she often complained about the fact that women were not allowed to become actors and appear on the stage for she felt that was where her real talents lay. Unfortunately she had fallen in love with the flamboyant Greene and there was little doubt he used her shamelessly to keep him in money for drink and gaming. But she was quick-witted and Simon liked her.

He found her in the Anchor Inn looking for the errant Greene. She was resigned to what Simon had to tell her about her wandering lover. 'I've been telling Robin for days he ought to come and see you, but you know what he is. Did he pay you?'

Simon shook his head. Emma looked in the purse at her waist and was about to take out some coins when Simon stopped her. 'Leave it, Emma, you can ill afford it. But there is something you can do for me.'

Emma gave him a broad smile for she had always found him attractive.

'Not that, Emma,' said Simon, smiling back. 'I want you to take a letter for me to a lady in the City. No,' he went on, seeing Emma's knowing look, 'it's not at all what you might think. All I can tell you, and I beg you to keep it to yourself, is that it concerns the dead girl recently found in the Thames near here. Perhaps you've heard of it. This letter is for the Lady Olivia Tuckett, the girl's mistress. There are good reasons why I can neither take it myself nor send my man. It's vital you find a way of giving it to her without anyone else's knowledge. She has both a husband and a father and there's also a sly secretary in the household eager to make mischief. Do you think you can do that?'

Emma listened, no longer smiling. 'It must be a very serious matter, Dr Forman,' she commented when he'd finished.

'Deadly serious. Not least because this lady's father has just done his best to deprive me of my livelihood.'

Emma was silent for a moment. 'The hard thing will be trying to see the lady by herself. If I just knock at the door with the letter it's most likely a servant will take it from me and it may never reach her. Or I could be sent about my business without even being able to do that. I need some other good reason and a suitable disguise. I can hardly go like this.' She indicated the brilliantly-coloured shabby gown she was wearing with its tarnished glitter. She paused for a moment then had an idea.

'My friend, Molly, sells lavender in the summertime. I saw her early this morning coming up the watersteps. She'd been up to the Wandsworth Fields at dawn and returned by boat with a whole tray of it which she's hoping will sell quickly since there's been so little lavender about because of the poor weather. I could ask her if she'd let me sell it for her in the City. She has no man and a young child dragging at her skirts. She might agree.'

Simon gave her some coins. 'Give her this and buy all she has left. If you can't see Lady Tuckett or she won't take it off you, then I certainly will. I can always make good use of it, it's one of the most valuable all-round herbs known to man, dried or distilled as oil. I'm sure I can leave it to you to ensure you look the part.'

'I'll do my best.'

He stooped and kissed her on the cheek. 'I'm most

grateful to you for doing this for me, Emma. Come to the house afterwards and let me know whether or not you succeeded.'

Emma returned to her little house and climbed the ladder staircase to the single bedroom in the eaves. Stepping over Robin's discarded and dirty doublets and hose, which lay all over the floor, she picked off a peg the cleanest and most respectable of a number of gowns, all of which had seen better days. She then washed her face, combed and pinned up her hair, even managing to find a linen cap to put on, arranged a dull grey shawl around her shoulders and peered into a piece of broken mirror to see the result. She decided it would do.

She found her friend sitting disconsolately at the Southwark end of London Bridge, a small girl grizzling beside her, and with most of her tray of lavender unsold.

'It's because it's too dear for most,' she complained. 'Folk are waiting for a few more days' sunshine when it'll be cheaper.' Not surprisingly she eagerly accepted Emma's offer to buy the whole tray off her 'for a doctor' and thankfully took her child back to their lodgings.

Emma was somewhat daunted by the grandeur of Sir Wolford's house, not least because she'd not expected a closed gate and a porter. She lurked in the shadows for what seemed an age until the gate was opened and an important-looking person in a furred gown swept out, accompanied by a dark young man carrying a large and bulging leather pouch over his shoulder. Once outside the two men turned right and made off in the direction of St Paul's.

She waited until they were out of sight then walked over and rang the bell. The porter gave her a disparaging look and asked what she wanted. She put on a humble expression and replied that she was here with the new season's lavender the mistress had asked her to bring. The man scratched his head, looked doubtful, and told her to wait where she was while he found out about it. Time passed and she was just about to ring again when he reappeared. 'No one knows anything about it,' he said. 'The servants think it must have been ordered by Lady Tuckett's maid on her behalf.'

'Can you not ask her then?' queried Emma, wondering what his response would be.

Her question brought him up short. 'She's . . . she's no longer here,' he replied in a tone which suggested that was the end of the matter. Emma was just wondering what she should do next when he added irritably, 'However the housekeeper says you've to come in and she'll enquire about it further.'

The porter took her round to the back of the house and left her outside in a small yard after telling her to wait exactly where she was while he went and fetched the housekeeper. Left alone, Emma began cautiously exploring her surroundings. To the right of the yard and its out-buildings was a small archway in the middle of a box hedge from which she could see an enclosed garden. She went over and peered through. A young, fair-haired woman in a green silk gown was sitting on a bench reading a book. Emma looked around. There was no sign of the porter or a housekeeper. Emboldened she entered the garden and approached the young woman, stopping a few feet away.

'Lady Tuckett?' she enquired.

Olivia looked up. 'Who are you?' she exclaimed in surprise. 'What are you doing here? Who let you in?'

Emma glanced back towards the house, terrified the sound of voices would bring people out to them, but all was quiet. She faced Olivia and curtsied. 'I've brought the lavender you wanted, madam.'

'I've ordered no lavender,' said Olivia. 'I don't know what game you're playing but you'd best be off before I call the servants to you.'

There was no help for it. It was now or never. Emma rooted under the lavender and brought out the letter which she thrust into Olivia's hand. 'It's from Dr Forman. He said I must be sure to give it to you when you're on your own. And that it's urgent.'

Olivia looked towards the house, broke the seal on the letter and rapidly read it. It was obvious its contents were unwelcome. She folded it and pushed it into the bodice of her gown. 'Tell Dr Forman I will meet him and that I'll send word as to the time and place as soon as I can.' She then looked at Emma with more interest. 'Are you one of his servants?'

Emma replied that she was not.

Olivia gave her a calculating look. 'His mistress then?'

'No, your ladyship, just a neighbour. My . . . my husband has been treated by Dr Forman.'

At that point the housekeeper, who had come to the back door and failed to find Emma, saw the two women together and called the servants. A young lad appeared immediately followed by the porter and all three began moving purposefully towards the archway, the porter shouting to Emma to 'come out of there at once!'

'They think your maid ordered the lavender,' said Emma, hurriedly, 'but said they couldn't ask her as she isn't here any more.'

Olivia made no response to this but when the three reached her, the housekeeper demanding that Emma tell her what she thought she was about thrusting herself on my lady in this pert fashion, Olivia quelled her.

'It's all right, Hannah. No harm's been done. The girl's ignorant and knows no better. I'd asked Eliza to find me fresh lavender when it was ready and it seems she asked this young woman to bring it to the house as soon as she had some.' Then she turned to Emma. 'Very well, my girl, you can give the lavender to my housekeeper and here's a coin for your trouble. But if you ever come again, wait where you're told to until you're sent for.'

Olivia then settled back in her seat, smoothed down her gown and picked up her book. 'Be off with you. And before you go, give Hannah your direction so that she can send to you if we need more.' Emma followed the housekeeper back down the path, told her where she lived and was then shown out of the gate by the porter who expressed his own opinion of her by slamming it behind her.

Back in the garden Olivia took the letter out and read it again. Then she threw it down and put her head in her hands.

Chapter 13

The Three Pigeons

Several days passed without Simon receiving any response to his letter. He did his best to settle back into as much of a routine as was possible given the fact that he could no longer visit patients on the north side of the river. In the mornings he caught up with his neglected Casebook notes, after which he saw to the needs of the inhabitants of the Bankside, the ulcers and chesty coughs, the wasting sickness and the fistulas, and pox and the clap and the horoscope-seekers, the latter providing him with his only decent fees.

It was nearly three weeks after Eliza's body had been taken from the river when Anna came in while he was writing up his case notes to say that a 'religious gentleman' was waiting in the hall to see him. He rose at once and went out to greet him to find that it was not a patient at all but Dr James Field, deep in a book. Simon greeted him warmly. 'It's a rare sight to find the word of God being read by someone waiting to see me, sir.'

Field smiled and stood up, returning his greeting. 'I fear I must confess to you, Dr Forman, that you are mistaken. This is a copy of Master Chapman's translation of Homer which I purchased yesterday. It is highly diverting.' Simon guided Field into his study, asking what had brought him to London.

'I had some business in the City,' he replied, 'and as my wife and daughters were eager to see something of town life we are all here, staying with an old colleague of mine near St Paul's. I also wanted to see you again, Doctor, as I have recently been visited by Mistress Pargeter who was in some distress.'

'I see,' responded Simon.

'She explained that you had asked her not to divulge what passed between you but she was finding it too large a burden to carry alone since she felt unable to confide in her family. I assured her, as I now do you, that it will go no further.' He stopped abruptly then said, 'Since we met, I have read the report of the Inquest proceedings. Tell me, Dr Forman, why did you not inform me that you suspect Eliza had met her death by foul means and that this had been the verdict of the jury?'

'To be frank, Dr Field, no sooner had I left you than I felt I should have done. But I was still unsure myself and as we'd never previously met I decided to keep it to myself. I'm aware I made the wrong decision.'

Field nodded. 'I realise you were in some difficulty. However, if what you told Mistress Pargeter is indeed true then it would appear that Sir Wolford Barnes and his family are involved in a heinous crime.'

'That is certainly what I believe,' said Simon.

'And your reasoning?'

'I'm still trying to piece it all together. Mistress Pargeter told you of the money Eliza received? So huge a sum for so young a girl. I see no reason for it other than that she was being paid for her silence, for not divulging something which would bring trouble or scandal on her mistress's family.'

'So resulting in her being made away with,' responded Field.

'Exactly.'

The clergyman considered this. 'But what of the child she was expecting? Could it be that of Sir Wolford himself, do you think, or of Sir Marcus?'

Simon admitted that he had been unable to come up with an answer.

'If not that,' continued Field, 'then what of this. This Lady Olivia must provide an heir, as you know. Is it not possible that some plan was afoot for her maid to bear a child which could be passed off as that of her mistress in the event she did not conceive one? It might be possible to carry out such a deception if she refused all marital relations with her husband from soon after the child was supposed to have been conceived, on the grounds that such activity might harm it.'

This was not an idea that had previously occurred to Simon. 'It's a possibility, I suppose,' he said, after some thought, 'although if Olivia Tuckett then also became with child it would seem to be not only unnecessary but fraught with complications.'

'Unless the child died or was stillborn. Such sad outcomes happen every day. And Sir Wolford is quite ruthless. I truly believe there are no lengths to which he would not go to hold on to the estate.'

'I scarcely need convincing of that,' said Simon and told Field of the attempt made to stop him attending the Inquest, followed by the way Sir Wolford had brought pressure to bear on the Royal College to revoke his licence.

Field sighed. 'I'm very sorry to hear it, Dr Forman, but can scarcely pretend surprise. It is particularly distasteful to me as my enquiries in London as to your direction resulted in my hearing much good of you, especially how you treat the sick poor without expecting payment.'

'The sick poor are soon likely to have to fend for themselves,' replied Simon grimly, 'for to help them I need the fees of the wealthy.'

Field rose. 'I must not keep you any longer from your work. I called merely to say that I am here and shall be in the City for at least another week. I will also make some enquiries of my own during that time. Perhaps we can meet again before I return to Stratford St Anne?'

Dr Field was not the only visitor. Later that day a young lad knocked on the door bearing a letter 'for the doctor'. It was from Olivia Tuckett.

'Dear Dr Forman,' she wrote. 'Arranging to see you has not been easy since I am expected to inform my father and husband wherever I go. However, my husband now wishes me to accompany him to Kent as his father is grievously sick. He leaves tomorrow and I've told him I'll join him a little later as there are a number of household matters which require my attention here first. Since it isn't possible for us to meet anywhere where either of us might be recognised, I propose we should do so at the

Three Pigeons in Brentford the day after tomorrow. I would ask that you come in the early evening. I have no lady's maid at present and will be attended only by a groom whom I will ensure is not party to our meeting – Olivia Tuckett.'

The lady's suggestion of the Three Pigeons raised a smile, for the inn was not only well-known for its considerable stables which enabled travellers to change horses with ease but had also acquired considerable notoriety as a place of assignation. It was therefore a shrewd move by Olivia to offer to meet him there, as presumably the landlord and his servants must be experts in discretion and used to holding their tongues when ladies and gentlemen arrived – and left – separately.

John Bradedge exploded when Simon told him he proposed to go to Brentford on his own. 'You're moon mad,' he told his master. 'Surely you see this strumpet's game? It won't be one cutthroat in an alley this time, it'll be half a dozen hefty fellows with knives and cudgels, or even pistols.'

Simon attempted to calm him down. 'I haven't quite lost my wits. I shall watch my back all the time and, yes, I'll take my rapier with me. I'll also tell the lady when we meet that I've left behind me in a safe place a note explaining where I've gone and details of my suspicions, along with her own letter. She'll hardly want to risk such documents coming to light.'

'But if you're murdered, who'll believe it?' countered John. 'And what place is safe enough from the likes of Sir Wolford Barnes? He'll invent some pretext to have the place searched wherever you hide them.'

'I will give you a package to take to Dr James Field. I understand he's staying with a canon of St Paul's, and even Sir Wolford is unlikely to persuade the authorities to search such a property. If it sets your mind at rest, when you give it to Field, tell him if I've not returned by the next morning and sent word to that effect, then he must open it and act as he sees fit.

John watched his master ride out to Brentford two days later and as soon as he was out of sight called to Anna that he was away to hire himself a decent horse and that she must have his boots, cloak and arms ready for him when he returned. 'I'll deliver the letter to the parson, then I'm off after him. He may have plenty of book learning and know all about the stars but he's no common sense when it comes to this kind of thing. You mark my words, he's riding straight into trouble!'

Half an hour later, having kissed Anna and little Simon farewell and telling his wife she'd no need to worry on his behalf, he trotted as briskly as he could over London Bridge, armed with a sword, a serviceable dagger and with a pistol in the pouch on his saddle.

Olivia arrived at the Thee Pigeons in a hired carriage in the middle of the afternoon, her groom sitting in front with the driver. The landlord was indeed the very soul of tact. Certainly the lady could have a private room, he had just the thing, very quiet and secluded and facing out over the garden at the back. She was expecting a gentleman? Ah, her brother was arriving later. He quite understood. Would her – brother – also be requiring a room? He managed not to smile when the lady informed him that only one room would be needed as it was unlikely he would be staying overnight. However she would like a good supper sent up for the two of them when he arrived, along with some of the inn's choicest wines. There was also a need for accommodation for her groom and the driver of her carriage. Again that was no problem. There was a large room over the stables for that very purpose in which they could each have a bed along with others of their kind.

As requested, Simon did not arrive in Brentford until considerably later. After leaving the Bankside he had passed through Blackfriars in search of the home of Olivia's friend, Celia Wynter, secure in the knowledge that his visit would not be reported to Olivia who was now safely in Brentford until the next day.

It took him only a short time to discover where the Wynters lived. The house was not as grand as that of Sir Wolford but it was evident that here too was wealth. He knocked on the door and waited in some trepidation but this time he was to be in luck for it was opened by a young maidservant who told him she would find out if the young mistress could see him. She returned almost immediately and asked him to step into the hall where a rather plain, but grandly dressed young woman stood waiting for him. She looked at him unsmilingly then asked briskly who he was and the nature of his business.

Simon felt that, in the circumstances, deception was justified. 'My name is John Bradedge,' he told her. 'A clerk to Sir Thomas Monkton who sat on the Inquest into the death of Eliza Pargeter, Lady Olivia Tuckett's lady's maid. Since the verdict was one of wilful murder it has been necessary to make enquiries.'

'I cannot see why I should be able to help you,' the girl replied. 'She was, as you say, maid to my friend, not to me.'

Simon tried again. 'We are seeking to discover when this sad event might have taken place and understand from Lady Tuckett that she did not realise the girl had gone until the morning her body was taken from the river, since she had stayed late with you the previous evening.'

Celia Wynter looked unconvinced. 'I still do not see what this has to do with me but, since you ask, I have cause to remember that Olivia did indeed spend that evening here since shortly after we had dined she fainted.' She paused for a moment, remembering the event. 'I have never known her do such a thing before. My mother wondered later if it might mean she was with child as she was not long married. When she recovered we naturally said she could pass the rest of the night here and that we could send a servant to tell her family what had happened, but she insisted on returning home, which she did, with two of our servants to see she got there safely.'

Simon thanked her, told her solemnly that he was sure Sir Thomas would be grateful for her help and left before she either asked him anything else or he was faced with some other member of the family. He was not sure how useful the exercise had been but at least it showed that Olivia's friend was prepared to support her story whether it was true or not.

By the time he arrived at the Three Pigeons his mind was in turmoil as he had spent most of the journey thinking about what he was going to say to Olivia.

There were still so many gaps in his knowledge that Simon could only hope that he'd be able to come up with a story sufficiently convincing not only to persuade her he had a case but to force some kind of confession out of her as well. His mind also ranged over other tantalising possibilities. In spite of everything he found Olivia devastatingly attractive and he wondered exactly what she had in mind by suggesting this particular rendezvous with its obvious implications.

As he rode into the busy stable yard, however, he had more immediate and practical considerations. For whom should he ask? Olivia would hardly have taken a room in the name of Lady Tuckett. But as he handed over his horse to an ostler, the landlord himself appeared beside him to ask in a low voice if he was the doctor whose sister had arrived earlier and was expecting him. Simon agreed that he was, hoping neither of them had made a mistake and that he wouldn't find himself in the wrong room making excuses to a buxom merchant's wife awaiting her brisk young lover.

Olivia was standing gazing out over the garden in the rapidly falling dusk. She was wearing a loose gown in her favourite green and she looked very beautiful. There was a tap at the door and two servants brought in a variety of dishes, some fruit and a carafe of fine wine along with several bottles and two glasses. Olivia thanked them and told them they need not remain as they could wait upon themselves. Having seen everything arranged to their satisfaction the servants withdrew, leaving the two alone.

'I trust you will have supper with me Dr Forman,' she said after greeting him formally. 'You have had to come a fair way.' Simon bowed and said he'd be delighted, meanwhile casting his eyes round the room.

'You may examine it closely,' said Olivia. 'There are no hidden closets or priests' holes, no alcoves covered by hangings. You may even look under the bed and in the linen chest if you're so minded.' She walked over to the door, turned the key in the lock and handed it to him. 'And to set your mind completely at ease you may take that. No one can then burst in on us unsuspected.'

He unbuckled his sword, leaving it in a corner where he could easily reach it, took off his coat and they both sat down opposite to each other at the small table. As they ate they were careful to talk only of the most general matters but Simon was acutely aware of her proximity. Could it be that she'd asked him out here to seduce him in a final attempt to stop his meddling? He looked surreptitiously at the bed, admitting to himself that the notion was a pleasurable one. Or, more to the point and as John Bradedge has warned him, had she (possibly in collusion with her husband and father) arranged for him to be ambushed in the dark on his way home? He took the wine she offered him and pledged her health. It was rich and red and reminded him of that which he'd drunk with the Reverend Field.

They finished their meal and reached for the fruit bowl. 'And now, Dr Forman,' said Olivia, 'perhaps you'll be so good as to tell me of this information you claim has come your way. I can't imagine what it might be.'

Simon sat back. 'It's hard to know where to start. However, I'll do my best. It exercised me where Eliza had entered the water, for she was hauled out a little down from Westminster and well above Blackfriars and London Bridge, and therefore she must have been put in or thrown in upriver. According to the wherryman who found her body, the most likely place was somewhere along Chelsea Reach. A few days ago I went out there and, walking by Chelsea Creek, discovered two interesting facts: that on the very same night that she drowned a boat belonging to one of the local boatmen was used without his knowledge and that, by a strange coincidence, your father owns farmland in that very area.'

She made to interrupt him but he motioned her to let him finish. 'I also have it on good authority that on the night Eliza died she was seen leaving your house riding pillion behind your father's secretary: that was the last time she was ever seen at all.'

Olivia laughed. 'Then it seems we've both gone to a great deal of inconvenience for nothing. Whoever is your informant is misleading you when they told you they'd seen Eliza riding off with Down the night she died. She had been missing all that day. As to stolen boats and my father's rents in Chelsea, it sounds the stuff of a playhouse plot. Is this truly all?' She poured him another glass of wine.

'Not quite.' Simon took it and drank. 'Your father, Lady Tuckett, has done his best to lose me my livelihood.

Therefore I've little else left to lose. So tell me, was it you or some other member of your household who gave Eliza Pargeter a hundred guineas some four months before she died?' He saw he had hit home and that she had not expected this. 'A generous gift, so much so that it leaves one asking the reason for such generosity.'

'And have you found one?' she countered although she was obviously shaken.

'I think you gave it to her in return for her silence on some matter of great concern. But that it proved insufficient and she asked for more as is not unusual in such cases. So other means had to be found to close her mouth.'

'This is even more like some popular drama. You should write for the stage.'

Simon pressed on. 'So what was Eliza to keep silent about? A family scandal?' Olivia said nothing but got up from the table and walked over to the window. She appeared to be considering the view of the garden. Simon remained where he was.

'When you called on me at my home and I opened the door of my study and saw you standing there in your grey dress, for a moment – and only for a moment – I thought you the ghost of Eliza Pargeter. Then it occurred to me to wonder if the root of this matter is to do with your having at least once changed places and impersonated each other for some compelling reason; in effect she became your changeling.'

Olivia turned and looked at him but she did not smile. 'There seems to be no end to your fantasies, Dr Forman.

If you start putting such stuff about you'll either be ridiculed or thought fit for the madhouse.'

'But it was the likeness, wasn't it?' repeated Simon, now convinced he was close to the truth. 'You changed places with Eliza – but for what?' He paused. Then suddenly Olivia's derisory reference to playhouse plots prompted the memory of the conversation he'd had with the actor, Thomas Pope, and it came to him in a flash of inspiration. 'It's the bed-switch plot! You're quite right. It *is* a plot for a playhouse!' He had developed an insatiable thirst and looked at his empty glass and the wine bottle. Olivia motioned him to take more and he picked up the bottle, offering it to her, but she declined and so he refilled his glass to the brim, then stood up and walked over to stand beside her.

This time it was obvious he had hit home. 'You must know the story,' he challenged, 'one girl changes places with another on the wedding night because she should have been his true bride or for fear of . . . for fear of what, Lady Tuckett?'

Olivia gave him her most brilliant smile. 'You'd best call me Olivia, Simon Forman, since we are now discussing such intimate matters. You ask what I was afraid of? Then I'll tell you. That my husband would discover my loss of virginity. Now are you satisfied?'

'So Eliza took your place? That was the bargain, wasn't it? One hundred guineas for your place in your husband's bed.' He stopped again. 'But of course! It didn't end there, did it? He got her with child. Did she then ask for more money? Threaten exposure? The one thing that didn't seem to fit the rest of the facts was her being with child. I went through a number of possibilities including even a tumble with your husband, but none of them seemed threat enough to merit her being permanently silenced.'

'This is very ingenious – Simon – but I think it unlikely you can prove any of it.'

'Maybe not but if I did publish it abroad, while there would certainly be some who indeed might think me fit for the madhouse, there would be many others in whom the story would raise doubts. The old adage "no smoke without fire" still runs true.' Simon was aware that the wine was beginning to take a hold and felt swept away on a tide of exhilaration. He wondered why he was still so thirsty and looked around for water but could see none. 'Eliza had you trapped, Olivia. Not only could she bleed you dry, she'd the power to expose you at any time by threatening to tell your husband how he'd been duped. You could deny it, of course, turn her out into the street in disgrace, but would it be enough? What doubts might it not raise in the minds of both your husband and your father? And so she was murdered,' he finished triumphantly.

Olivia's face turned grey and she seemed about to faint as her mind returned to the ingenious idea that had led her to this point . . .

She had realised for some time beforehand of course that she would have to marry, not least to secure her father's estate, although the selection of idiots he presented to her as possible husbands had made her heart sink. But Olivia knew her duty was to provide her family with a male heir before Sir Wolford's death since he had patently failed to do so. Also he was becoming weary of her rejection of every suitor offered to her, even going so far as to remind her pointedly that she was no longer in the first flush of youth and her choice might well diminish further if she left it any longer. She also had reasons of her own. The affair she had eagerly entered into with Francis Down, so all-consuming to begin with, had gone sour after she conceived his child. But he refused to accept the end of it, continually pressing her to bed with him again, at one point threatening exposure. A husband, therefore, seemed a good way of ending her involvement with him once and for all.

It was at this point she finally agreed to marry Sir Marcus Tuckett. He was no better and no worse than many another contender, and he had the considerable advantage of being heir to a distinguished title. So the lawyers proceeded to draw up the marriage settlement and the amount of her dowry was agreed along with the generous allowance which was to be settled on the young couple. Sir Marcus would of course inherit his family's run-down and heavily-mortgaged estates on his father's death, but in spite of the fact that substantial sums of Sir Wolford's money would now be available to start putting the Tuckett house and lands into some sort of order, Lord Tuckett's lawyer was unhappy that the future of Sir Wolford's considerable country property was dependent on the new Lady Tuckett producing a son. However in the end it was agreed that it was unlikely so robust a young woman would fail to breed and so a date was set for the wedding some four weeks later.

It was at the dinner given by Sir Wolford to mark the couple's formal betrothal that old Lord Tuckett had drunk the health of the prospective bride, shouting out that he envied his son so delectable a virgin, adding in jest that at least he trusted she was a virgin. At this Marcus, flushed now with wine, had smiled at her rather unpleasantly and said that he was certainly experienced enough to know if she was not. The look he gave her had been a calculating one. Thankfully the uncomfortable moment soon passed in a welter of bawdy jests from the rest of the guests but the incident had left Olivia feeling cold.

Naturally she had realised that virginity was expected of her but she was hardly the first bride to go to the altar without it, and had been prepared to deal with any problems that might arise as best she could when the time came. But the Tucketts had been very definite. Just what would Marcus Tuckett expect in the way of proof? Later that night, unable to sleep, she had lit her candle and picked up a book of Italian tales with which she had been diverting herself for several weeks. It was then she saw a possible way out of her dilemma.

The morning after the brilliant idea had come to her she broached the subject to Eliza while the girl was dressing her hair. Because of the results of her previous liaison, her maid obviously knew she'd had at least one lover and might well have been aware that it was Francis Down, although, even in the depths of Olivia's anguish resulting from the consequences of the old woman's potion, she'd said nothing. The question of how she might pass herself off as a virgin on her wedding night therefore needed little explanation.

Eliza, as expected, was extremely practical. 'Surely you can fool a great gabey like him. Fill him up with wine enough and he'll not know anything about it come the morning. I'd a friend back home who did just that. Her man rolled into bed insensible and all she'd to do was nick her finger and rub it on the bedsheet then tell him the next day he'd been at it half the night.'

'But what if he obstinately refuses to get drunk?' queried Olivia. 'It might well be. His father made much of my being a virgin leading Sir Marcus to inform all present he'd certainly know if I wasn't!'

Eliza finished Olivia's hair and went to fetch the ruff to go with her gown. When she returned Olivia put the proposition to her. Eliza was much of her height and build. Supposing, just supposing, it was possible for them to change places on the wedding night?

Eliza looked doubtful. 'But how could that work? You'll both be put to bed by the wedding guests with all to see and when they've gone he might want his pleasure straight off and with all the candles lit.'

Olivia had already considered that. 'I'll ensure we have the grand guest chamber for the bridal night. As you know there's a closet close to the bed. After the guests have left us, I'll insist I must use the close-stool after so much rich food and wine and so slip into it. I'll also play the true virgin and say he must bed me in the dark. I'll ensure all my gowns and cloaks are hanging in the closet so that you can conceal yourself behind them. You will then get into the bed instead of me and remain with him until he falls asleep. When he does, we'll change places again.' Then a sudden thought struck her. 'You *are* a virgin, aren't you Eliza?'

Eliza responded with her cool smile. 'Oh yes, mistress. I've had no inclination to be otherwise. But what if he doesn't fall asleep afterwards?'

'We must give him something to make sure he does, something that can be put into wine. You must find a physician some distance from here and tell him I'm having trouble sleeping and am in need of a draught. Then all we need do is put it into some wine and see to it that he drinks it. I know I'm asking a great deal of you,' she continued in some desperation, for Eliza said nothing, 'but I'll make it well worth your while. A good dowry will easily find you a husband. If you'll do this for me I'll give you more money than you've ever dreamed of. Tell me, what would you think a fair sum?'

Eliza looked at her levelly with those calculating light eyes. 'A hundred guineas.'

A hundred guineas had been a large price to pay but Olivia was desperate and so it was agreed. Three days later Eliza had returned with a small phial of poppy syrup purchased from a physician on the Bankside. Olivia looked at it doubtfully wondering out loud if the amount were sufficient.

'I did ask for more, mistress, but he said he wouldn't give it me but would need to see you himself as the mixture was strong and should only be taken with care.'

'You didn't tell him who I was?' she asked in alarm.

Eliza reassured her. 'Of course not, in fact I made out it wasn't really the poppy syrup I'd come about. You see the doctor also casts horoscopes and so I asked him to cast mine. Only afterwards did I ask for a sleeping draught.'

'And did he cast your horoscope?' asked Olivia.

'He did but told me to come back in a few days as it takes time. If you don't think this is enough and he won't give me any more, I'll see what I can do to get it anyway.'

Olivia was intrigued. 'And who is this doctor of medicine who casts horoscopes?'

'He's called Dr Simon Forman.'

The name meant nothing to her and Olivia soon forgot it as preparations for the wedding continued at an accelerating pace. A few days before, Eliza told her she thought she'd found a way of acquiring some more poppy syrup but would need money to do so. Later that same day she returned with it, saying nothing of how it had been achieved. Nor did she mention the result of her horoscope.

Even if relations between church and manor house had been other than they were, the wedding would have taken place in the City. Sir Wolford was determined it should be an event of the utmost splendour to demonstrate his wealth and importance to all around him, his daughter as its centrepiece. Her gown, on which a team of sempstresses had worked, was of cloth of silver embroidered with pearls (for purity) and trimmed with the finest lace money could buy. She would be attended to the altar by no less than six bridesmaids all dressed in white brocade. Other needlewomen were brought in to see to the bridal linen and to make shifts, petticoats and nightshifts. Of the latter Olivia had insisted on two of them being made to exactly the same pattern.

On the morning of her wedding day her father and mother came to her chamber to wish her well and her father gave her a fine pendant bearing his coat of arms in small jewels. Shortly before noon Olivia was taken to the church in a carriage decked with white ribbons and garlands, her hair, unbound and down her back as a token of maidenhood, crowned with white flowers. She remembered little afterwards of the ceremony from which she emerged as Lady Tuckett, her mind being almost entirely taken up with what lay ahead.

The celebrations as was usual went on for many hours, the lavish hospitality continuing into the evening when the feasting and drinking gave way to dancing and horseplay. When to put a happy couple to bed varied, usually depending on how they themselves felt about it: those who had lusted after each other for months would make the move as soon as was decently possible while others, who felt either apprehensive or indifferent to what was in store, tended to spin the festivities out as long as they could. It seemed Olivia fell into the latter category as she showed no sign of wishing to leave the party although her bridegroom was becoming increasingly impatient. While Sir Marcus had drunk a great deal of wine it was clear he was far from being drunk and incapable.

Finally unable to put it off any longer, Olivia signalled

that the time had come. Attended by her bridesmaids and other female guests she was taken to the bridal chamber where her magnificent wedding gown was unlaced and the heavy farthingale removed along with her petticoats. Eliza had laid one of the fine nightshifts on the bed and this she now put on to much giggling banter about how long it would be before her new husband removed it. One of the girls asked whether Eliza herself would be sleeping with the other servants below stairs as Olivia would not be needing her that night. As Olivia climbed into the great bed she saw with satisfaction that Eliza had put a carafe of wine and a glass beside the bed next to a branch of candles.

A noise from outside heralded the arrival of the bridegroom, now in a bedrobe, led in by a noisy troop of young men who stood around while he climbed into bed beside Olivia to much explicit advice as to how he should set about what came next. The bride then threw her ribbon garters to the girls who struggled with each other to catch them and thus discover who should marry next, and finally, after what seemed to Olivia an age, the whole party noisily withdrew leaving the couple alone. Marcus wasted no time. As soon as the door closed he threw off his robe, knelt across her and pushed his hand up her shift. It was obvious he had no time for any niceties. But she struggled away from him.

'What now?' he demanded. 'You've already kept me waiting for hours.'

She put on what she hoped was a seductive smile. 'I've eaten and drunk too well, I fear. Before we . . . before there is more, forgive me but I must use the close-stool.'

'Be quick about it then,' he grumbled as she got out of bed.

'There's wine for you there,' she told him, pointing to it, 'the finest canary wine.' He gave it a cursory glance and told her he'd drink it later. As she passed him she snuffed out the candles.

'What've you done that for?' he asked in exasperation.

'To spare my blushes,' she replied and swiftly entered the closet now dimly lit by a single candle.

Eliza was waiting for her dressed in an identical night-shift, shivering with a mixture of cold and trepidation now it had actually come to the point. Silently Olivia made it clear that all was going well then, remembering that she was still wearing her father's wedding gift, removed the pendant and slipped it over the girl's head. Her heart thudded as Eliza crept away then she closed the closet door not wanting to hear what would come next.

It seemed a very long time before the girl returned, her face set, her shift torn. She was very pale. 'You can go to him now,' she said, 'he drank the wine and now he's asleep, snoring like a hog.'

Olivia began to whisper her thanks.

Eliza stopped her. 'It was a bargain between us, mis-tress, and I've kept my side of it. Never fret. He's none the wiser. Don't they say all cats are grey in the dark?'

Once her wedding night was over without incident and with no sign that Marcus was aware of the trick played on him, Olivia paid Eliza the promised sum. It had not been at all easy to raise the hundred guineas for she'd little or no access to money of her own and while before her marriage she had always been able to coax modest sums from her father, she could hardly apply to him now for a sum very far from modest, and even if she had summoned up the courage to do so he would have made it clear that it was for her husband to provide for her needs now. After all it was Sir Wolford's money which was propping up the Tucketts.

The only way she could keep her side of the bargain therefore was to recourse to selling some of her jewellery. She looked through the contents of her jewel case considering which pieces were least likely to be missed. There was a rather fine hair ornament set with pearls, a present from her parents on her fifteenth birthday, and an ugly but ornate jewelled bracelet which had been a bequest from a great aunt. But how was she to set about selling them? She knew most of the jewellers in the City and was unable to imagine what possible reason she could offer for selling two such valuable pieces. Worse, any one of them might well decide her father ought to know what his daughter was doing. More problems would arise if she sent a servant to carry out the transaction, for any reputable jeweller would refuse to believe such fine pieces had not been stolen.

So it was that after successfully keeping Francis Down at arm's length since she had rid herself of his child, she finally felt she had no other recourse but to turn to him for help and confess why she needed the money. He had listened to her without interruption, his eyes narrowed and calculating.

'Was there no other way? You took an almighty risk.'

'Do you think I don't know that?' she cried.

'And what if Tuckett discovers even now that he was fooled? You'll be shamed beyond redemption.'

'But he hasn't discovered it, nor will he,' she assured Down with growing confidence. 'As to some other way, yes, possibly I might have convinced him of my virginity by writhing and crying out but he made so much of his knowledge in this particular that I didn't dare leave it to chance. And why rail at me?' she continued bitterly. 'Had I not given myself to you, the question would never have arisen.'

'How so?' He smiled at her in the knowing way she now found deeply unpleasant. 'Do you forget there was another before me?' She turned away from him and he put a hand on her arm. 'Look at me, Olivia. Don't you realise what you've done? You say there's no way Tuckett will ever know but how can you be sure? Eliza has you now in her pocket.'

'Eliza's loyal and can be trusted.'

'She's had no reason until now to be anything but loyal and trustworthy. Oh, I agree she's been a model lady's maid and everything you could wish, but I've long thought that behind that cool exterior and modest demeanour lies a ruthless young woman. Believe me, lady, I can recognise in others what I see in myself. You've given Eliza something she's never had before: power. It's a heady drug. At the very least it might develop in her a taste for asking for money.'

Olivia brushed his hand away. 'You're talking nonsense.

She has an excellent position here, far better than many other girls of her age and station in life and if she's as shrewd as you claim, then she's unlikely to want to jeopardise it. Besides, the money will virtually buy her a husband of her choice when she chooses to wed.'

He took the two pieces of jewellery and put them in his pocket. 'Don't say I didn't warn you.'

Olivia viewed him with increasing impatience. 'Sell the jewellery and bring me the money to give to her and that will be the end of it. That was the bargain. Her place in my bridal bed for a hundred guineas. There is nothing more.'

Just over two months later Eliza came to her mistress one morning and told her she was certain she was with child.

As the memories of what had taken place flooded back to her now, Olivia swayed towards Simon in the room in the Three Pigeons and he rushed to catch her. She began to shake and then burst into tears. 'I never intended her death,' she sobbed. 'I was quite desperate, but I never thought of ending her life as a way out. Why did I ever confide in Francis Down!'

'The sly secretary. I see.'

'I'd no one in whom I could confide. I didn't know what to do for it was obvious that however much money I gave Eliza she'd come back for more. I turned to Francis Down in desperation. He had always . . . admired me. He comforted me and said he would deal with the matter and I must think no more of it. When Eliza disappeared I assumed he'd resolved things satisfactorily, had found a way of convincing her that she must leave London for good. I hoped she'd gone back home. I was as shocked as anyone when you came to tell us she'd been found in the Thames.'

Simon began to feel very strange. The whole situation was becoming quite unreal. Everything seemed to be taking place at a distance, as if he were a spectator watching some unknown man and woman through thick glass. It was an effort even to talk, let alone think, but finally he managed to ask, 'Did you then ask Down what had happened?'

She nodded. 'He denied it, of course. He said that he'd merely given her a choice: that she swear never to raise the matter ever again and return home at once or he would see to it that she was disgraced and whipped at the cart's tail and put in Bridewell as a lying whore.'

She was obviously desperate that he should believe her. She turned towards him and suddenly laid her head on his shoulder. A wisp of scented hair brushed his face. He gulped down the rest of the wine and put the glass down. Perhaps after all she was telling the truth. He was finding it more and more difficult to concentrate, to marshal his thoughts. She lifted her face to his and he kissed her. She kissed him back with real passion then clung to him. Over her shoulder the lights of the candles danced before his eyes.

'You don't have to leave,' she said very softly, then with more urgency, 'don't go! It's late now and no one will ever know. Please don't leave me.'

They walked over to the bed across a floor which Simon found increasingly unstable. He sat down heavily, tugging off his boots. The room seemed to be turning round as he clambered on to the bed. Olivia came towards him slipping off her robe as she did so. If only his mouth wasn't so appallingly dry. What he needed most of all was a drink. A drink . . . what was it about a drink?

'My God!' He tried to sit up but found he was unable to do so. He struggled to get the words out. 'The poppy syrup . . . so much . . . poppy syrup.' It was the last thing he said.

Chapter 14

In Hazard

John Bradedge reckoned Simon must have reached the Three Pigeons a good couple of hours before he did as he had a faster horse. As he left his own in the stables, he saw Simon's mare in a stall munching on some fodder. The inn was a busy one and, yet again, he found himself sitting in a strange taproom waiting for something to happen. Time passed and he ordered some supper. He wondered how long Simon's tête-à-tête with Lady Tuckett would take and where they were in so rambling a place.

It began to get dark and a lad came round and lit candles in metal sconces. Twice John went outside in case Simon had left without his knowing, but the horse was still there. It really was getting very late. Perhaps there was an obvious, if not respectable, reason for the delay knowing the doctor's weakness where women were concerned. The woman might be a ladyship but she was still a woman. Perhaps her husband had proved unsatisfactory and she felt like a change, perhaps the secret assignation had itself been sufficient excuse. John sighed. It looked like being a long night.

As soon as Simon was safely unconscious, Olivia dressed

herself more practically and crept out of the room and down the backstairs to the stable yard where she summoned an ostler and told him to fetch her groom at once. She had changed her plans and they were to leave for home.

A few minutes later she was joined back at the room by Francis Down dressed as a groom. 'All's well then?'

She nodded. 'He's dead asleep. He knew much and guessed even more. I tried to convince him he was mistaken but he didn't believe me.'

Down went over to Simon and raised one of his eyelids. 'Well, that's all one now. I'll have the driver get the carriage ready then we'll get him into it telling the landlord he's dead drunk. He shouldn't wake up but have you something with which I can tie his hands should he wake?' She took off her girdle and he rolled Simon on his side and expertly tied his hands behind his back. 'I'll be back shortly. Have you money to pay the reckoning?' Wordlessly she handed him her purse. 'I'll pay it then and tell the landlord we're all leaving together. You get in the carriage with him and I'll ride out on his horse.'

He was soon back. He and the driver of the carriage hauled Simon off the bed and forced his boots back on, then Olivia went ahead while they supported Simon down the stairs, Down having taken the precaution of soaking him with wine to give credence to the story. There was some amusement from the sleepy ostlers, one of whom asked whether or not the gentleman had been able to achieve the purpose of his visit before drink rendered him insensible. Down, when he paid the reckoning, had told the landlord he would be riding 'his master's horse' home himself and it was saddled up and waiting when they reached the carriage. Simon was bundled into it, followed by Olivia. The driver cracked his whip and the carriage moved briskly out of the inn yard, Down following behind.

Once out of sight of the inn the driver stopped the carriage and Olivia got out. Down dismounted from Simon's horse and handed her the reins. 'Ride as fast as you can. I bribed the porter before we left and he'll be waiting to let you in at the yard gate. Get him to stable the horse, after which it's up to you. If you're seen, you must find some excuse for being up so early. I'll be back as soon as I can.' Kilting up her skirts to enable her to ride astride, Olivia set off as fast as she could for London.

John Bradedge woke from a doze to find the taproom almost empty. He was cold and stiff. Rousing himself, he went outside and then cursed himself for a lazy fool. Simon's horse had gone. He went back into the inn and found the sleepy innkeeper clearing away dirty tankards.

'I'm looking for my master,' he told him, 'but it seems he's gone.'

'Plenty of people have come and gone while you've been here,' the landlord replied.

'He came early. Before me. A gentleman with auburn hair and a small beard, well dressed and of middle height.' The landlord looked blank. John adopted a man-to-man tone. 'He came to meet a lady in a private room.'

The landlord gave a knowing wink. '*That* gentleman! Well I don't know if he satisfied the lady but he certainly satisfied himself with my wine. His servants have just taken him off home too drunk to stand. It's as well the lady had a carriage for he couldn't even walk down the stairs but needed two of them to prop him up. The younger man says it often happens as he can't hold his liquor; but you must know all that.'

John went cold. 'How long ago was this?'

'No more than twenty minutes, I'd say,' said the landlord.

'And which way did they go?'

'What way would they go but back to his home? They took the road by the river to Mortlake!'

The road to London was long and Olivia's thoughts crowded in on her. This was now the second time she'd been privy to murder. She felt sorry for Simon for her attraction to him was genuine and in other circumstances she would have been happy to enjoy herself in bed with him, indeed she'd been quite prepared to do so if the poppy syrup, combined with a good deal of wine, hadn't made it unnecessary. But he posed too much of a threat. She couldn't tell whether or not he really believed the explanation she had given of her part in Eliza's death, but she was sure that once his head cleared he would either insist on speaking to her again, or far worse, go direct to her father and husband. They too might well think drastic action was needed to get rid of Forman but they might also believe what he said. She was still not out of the labyrinth, and worse, was more than ever in debt for her survival to Francis Down.

But what else could she have done? When she'd told him that Eliza was with child by Sir Marcus and demanding more money, he was unsurprised. 'You wouldn't be told, would you? I warned you what would happen. Not the child, of course, I can't pretend I foresaw that, but about the rest I certainly did.'

'But what I told you was true,' she wailed, 'she'd been so loyal.'

Down ran his finger down the back of her neck. 'The lure of gold changes everything. Fortunately, my lady, I don't find it as seductive as other commodities. If you seek my help again, you know my price.'

They hatched the plan between them. Olivia was to appear to agree to Eliza's demand telling her she should have her money but that it would take a little while. That, they felt, should give them time to find a suitable opportunity to do what had to be done. This time, Down told Olivia, she'd better listen to him.

'Eliza must be given no hint that she's in any danger or she's certain to carry out her threat. Don't let any past fondness stand in the way now: you can't let your heart rule your head.'

Although Olivia had not seriously considered murder as a solution and was chilled by the matter of fact way Down was prepared to go about it, she knew there was no alternative unless she was prepared to live under permanent threat. For if Eliza ever carried it out and succeeded in convincing Marcus that she, not Olivia, had been his 'bride' on his wedding night and was now expecting his child when Olivia was not, there was little doubt Marcus would put her from him in the most public manner. The ensuing scandal, which would rebound on her father, would be sensational, and his reaction something she scarcely dared contemplate.

'Do you want to know what I intend or do you prefer to remain ignorant?' Down had asked her. She made no reply. 'Very well, for the time being do exactly as I tell you. The fact that she's having a child plays into our hands. If it can be made to look as if she took her own life then it will provide sufficient reason. It'll be just another tale of an innocent girl duped by a faithless lover.'

'What if it isn't noticed?' Olivia asked.

He thought for a moment. 'We'll put a piece of your jewellery in her pocket so that it'll be thought she thieved it. And do you have any of the poppy syrup left from your wedding night?'

'Eliza went back for more. There's plenty.'

'Keep it safe then.' He pulled her hard towards him. 'Your husband's at the gaming house, your father in the City and the house is quiet.' Expertly he began to unlace her bodice with his free hand. 'You and I, lady, are for bed.'

Three weeks after she had resumed her relationship with Down, it was clear Eliza was becoming increasingly restive. An opportunity had to be found and soon. It was Marcus who gave it to them. He came in one afternoon, flushed from gaming and wine, and told Olivia he was invited to Hertford the following day for there was to be a sporting meeting with wrestling, cock-fighting and bear-baiting, and that he assumed she'd not want to accompany him. She shuddered and said she most certainly did not. She had no wish to spend the day in the kind of sporting company he kept.

'Excellent,' said Down when she told him, 'luck's on our side. As you know, your father's planning a new joint venture to the Indies with Sir Henry Clavell and he's been invited down to Clavell's house near Barnes tomorrow to discuss it with several other venturers, to be followed by a grand dinner. He's planning to stay overnight. Tell Eliza you'll have the money for her tomorrow evening. Then, when both your father and husband have left, you and I will apparently ride out together on a jaunt.'

She looked puzzled. 'Whatever for?'

'So that I can return later and tell her you've suffered an accident – been thrown off your horse, say – and aren't severely injured but are unable to ride and so have sent me to fetch her. And that she must tell no one as Sir Marcus would be angry if he knew we'd ridden off alone together.'

'And what of me?'

'You can surely find a friend to visit and stay late? Feign a slight indisposition if it helps you to do so. I'll engage to have Eliza away by about ten o'clock. You can then return home in all innocence.'

She looked doubtful. 'It seems very risky.'

'Have you a better idea?' he retorted. 'No? Then we must hope our luck holds.'

'Where will you take her?'

'To Chelsea Creek. I'll tell her the accident happened near your father's farm and that you're waiting for her at the farmhouse. I'll take her pillion, stop on the way for refreshment, and give her enough of the drug to make her sleepy. Then I'll take her up before me to ensure she doesn't fall on the way.' He looked at her neck. 'Give me your pendant. We must have something valuable to be found on her.'

'But it was my father's wedding gift, it was made especially for the occasion.'

'All the more reason for her to run away if she stole it.'

Reluctantly she handed it to him, along with a phial of poppy syrup. Down stowed both away with care. 'Be friendly to the girl. Say that having thought about it, you might well take her back after the child is born so long as she goes to the country to deliver it and finds herself a docile husband. Leave the rest to me.'

'What are you going to do?' she asked.

'Take her out on the river and push her in upstream. If she's found, it'll be assumed she drowned herself.'

It had all seemed so simple. But now here she was, riding hell-for-leather along the dark road, with a second killing on her conscience.

Simon struggled into consciousness. He felt very sick, had pains in his head and when he surfaced sufficiently to try and move his arms he discovered they were tied behind his back. He also appeared to be covered by a thick and evil-smelling blanket. He must keep awake. He was obviously lying on the floor of some kind of carriage for he could feel it bumping under him and the noise of its wheels on the road. He cursed comprehensively. It was the second time John Bradedge had been right. At the very least he should have heeded his man's advice enough to take him along with him, instead of convincing himself that so long as he took elementary precautions there was little Olivia could do by herself.

But it was now all too obvious that she'd not been by herself. The fact that there was no one concealed anywhere in the room or lurking behind the door meant nothing. Worst of all he'd been so crassly stupid as to drink, actually *drink* wine laced with his own poppy syrup! Why on earth hadn't he recognised its sickly taste, his symptomatic dry mouth? She must somehow have added it to the wine a little at a time when she poured it for him, then left the rest in the bottle for him to help himself. He was unable to remember when she might have found the opportunity, for the events of the evening were hazy. Of one thing he was certain: that when she'd overtly invited him into bed, he'd been only too eager to accept and that the growing possibility she would do so had led him to throw all caution to the winds. Oh God, he'd give anything, anything to stop the pounding in his head.

After a little while he felt the carriage halt and heard a man say he'd best check the fellow was still asleep. He wondered if he was talking to Olivia. Would she go so far as to actually participate in his death? For he was certain now that was what was intended. Again he cursed himself for a stupid fool for putting his life in hazard. For what? An hour's pleasure with a scheming strumpet? He heard footsteps coming round the side of the vehicle then the door opened and someone climbed in. Simon lay perfectly still and breathed as steadily as he could as the blanket was pulled off his face and the man rolled him over with his foot.

'No sign of life,' the man called out to his companion. Simon was almost certain it was Francis Down. Had he really begun to believe Olivia was the secretary's almost-innocent victim? That she had turned to him driven by desperation and despair? They must both have been involved right from the start and had probably been, or still were, lovers. Down tugged at the cords round his arms to make sure they were still secure, then kicked him hard in the side; it was all Simon could do not to cry out. Down left the carriage, climbed up in front and rejoined the driver. 'Walk on. Turn off down the lane here on the left and go as near the river as you can, then we'll get it over with.'

Simon struggled frantically with the ropes round his arms and wrists without success. It seemed he was bound for the same fate as Eliza. If they did intend to drown him, would his bonds be cut before they did so as were hers? Perhaps Down, to make absolutely sure, intended to knife him first. He felt the carriage leave the lane for a rutted track, its wheels creaking as it lurched from side to side. Then it stopped again. It was quiet except for the sound of an owl hooting, so quiet that Simon, straining his ears, thought for a moment he heard the sound of a horseman some way behind but was unable to tell whether it was real or all in his head. Oh God, his head, if only he could think clearly. He made a mental note never, never again to sell anyone poppy syrup; in future he would only dispense it when he was able to ensure its proper use. Then he gave a wry smile; it was all academic since he was unlikely to survive to do so.

He heard Down and the driver get down from the driving seat. Presumably Olivia was not present after all. There was a brief pause then he heard the secretary curse.

'I thought there'd be more water than this. Oh well, we'll just have to make the best of it and wade in and push him out as far as we can.'

So he was right. It was to be the river. The whole sad tale had been inextricably entangled with London's great waterway from the discovery of Eliza's body to this final act.

'I never said I'd do more than drive this carriage,' replied the driver in a tone of unconvincing bravado. 'There was never no mention of a killing.'

'It makes no odds, you've been paid well enough,' Down replied.

'Not well enough for that. I'm off,' said the driver in rising panic. There was the sound of running feet, followed by a scuffle and the driver cried out.

'Get to your feet, fool.' Down sounded slightly breathless. 'This is my dagger pricking into your ribs. Make any more trouble and I'll kill you too. In fact it would suit me very well. I could stab you both and make it look as if he'd fought you off and killed you but that you'd fatally wounded him in the process. Stop snivelling and help me get him out.'

He opened the carriage door and they pulled Simon out by his feet, his head banging on the steps of the carriage, then they laid him on the grass. A horse neighed some way away.

'What's that?' quavered the driver.

'A horse. What do you think it is? It must be in a nearby field.'

Down knelt and raised Simon's eyelid and appeared satisfied. 'It's more potent stuff than I'd realised,' he told the driver. 'You take his feet and I'll take his head and let's get him down the bank.' Between them they struggled down with him to the water's edge. He could hear the sound of running water, presumably from a stream. The river gave off a dank smell.

'Now,' said Down, 'we'll have to get him across this mud. Whatever you do, don't let him go.'

They heaved Simon off the bank and he felt them struggle as their feet sank in the sticky mud. They began hauling him towards the water with obvious difficulty. The driver slipped and dropped his legs, causing Down to let go of his head. Simon felt the mud close over his nose and mouth and was fearful he'd suffocate before they pulled him free, but they both regained their grip and after a few minutes it was clear they were moving through water. Soon he felt it lapping round his head.

'Right,' said Down, struggling for breath, 'I'll cut his bonds and then we'll shove him out as far as we can.'

'Aren't you going to knock him on the head or something?' asked the driver.

'Not if I can help it. I'd rather there weren't any signs of foul play and in his state he should drown naturally.' Down laughed. 'At least this time he won't be around to cite rope marks and cry murder.' He turned Simon over so that he lay with his face in the river as he cut through his bonds. As Down made to turn him round and push him out into the current, Simon came suddenly to life and tried to grapple with him, but he was at a desperate disadvantage. There was nothing to give him leverage to raise himself in the soft mud and the more he tried to do so, the deeper he sank into it. He was also still slow-witted from the poppy syrup.

'Hell and damnation,' cursed Down, himself slipping on the mud then, to the driver, 'don't just stand there, for God's sake, push his head down in the water while I finish him off!' He raised his dagger and Simon closed his eyes waiting for the stroke. Instead there was a loud splashing in the shallows, followed by a shout, and his would-be murderer crashed down into the mud and water on top of him. Then came the sound of a pistol shot and the driver screeched. John Bradedge had arrived.

After being told that Simon had already left, he had flung himself on to his horse and raced out of the inn yard leaving the ostlers shaking their heads over the strange way folk behave. He was not at all sure where he was or even the direction of Mortlake, since he had never before been so far upriver, but if the doctor's theory was correct and Eliza had been thrown into the river to drown then it seemed likely that whoever was responsible was quite capable of trying the same trick again.

When he reached the place where the main road divided he was in luck for there he met a horseman coming the other way and asked him if he'd seen a carriage. The man said he had and that it had been travelling the opposite way in the direction of Mortlake but that before that he had almost been knocked off the road by a mad horseman riding like the devil. John thanked him and set off at a canter, grateful the road had a grassy verge which muffled the sound of his horse's hooves. Shortly afterwards he heard carriage wheels ahead of him and was just able to rein-in as it stopped. He waited where he was, terrified of giving himself away, until it turned off the road and down towards the river. He then followed at a discreet distance, arriving just in time to see his master about to be murdered.

He now heaved Down off Simon, then hauled the latter to his feet, dripping with mud and water. Simon clung to his rescuer, gasping for air. 'Thank God you disobeyed me. Without you I'd be dead.'

'You most certainly would, Doctor.' John had every reason to sound satisfied and could not resist adding, 'I did tell you what would happen, didn't I?'

'You did and I can only thank you from the bottom of my heart for being such a true friend.' Simon looked down at his attacker lying in the mud, the water having receded further during the struggle. 'What did you do to him?'

'Knocked him on the head with my sword hilt though I'd not have thought twice at running him through.'

'And what was the shot?'

'The driver was going to run off so I told him not to move and fired over his head to show him I meant what I said. Here you,' he called to where a dim shape could be seen beside a bush, 'come and help us unless you want me to put my next shot through you.'

The driver, by this time scared witless, promptly came and did as he was told, and with difficulty they dragged Francis Down back up the bank.

'Have I killed him?' John enquired.

'I doubt it.' Simon knelt beside Down and examined him. 'He's got a nasty deep cut where the hilt went into his scalp and you've rendered him unconscious, but he'll live to be hanged.' He stood up, swaying on his feet. 'No,' he said in answer to John Bradedge's unspoken question, 'I'm not really hurt, it's just cuts and bruises and I'm stiff. But they drugged me and the effects still haven't worn off.' He turned to the driver and pointed to Down. 'If you don't want to end up hanging beside him at Tyburn, then you'll do exactly as you're told. We'll take him back to London with us to my house. I'll travel inside to make sure we get him there, we'll hitch my man's horse on behind and John'll sit beside you – with his pistol.' The mention of the horse reminded him. 'My horse. I left it at the inn.'

'It seems one of them took it, Doctor,' said John. 'Leastways that's what I was told and it wasn't there when I looked.'

'Ah, well, we'll have to try and find out what happened to it tomorrow – or rather, later today. So it's back to the Bankside. We'll put this fellow somewhere where he can't make any trouble, clean ourselves up, have a rest, and then I think we'll ask Dr Field if he'd be so kind as to accompany us all to the home of Sir Wolford Barnes.'

Chapter 15

Endgame

By the time Olivia reached the outskirts of the City she was exhausted and shivering with cold. An early dawn was breaking as she rode towards Bishopsgate but at least she could be confident that no one that mattered would be home to comment on her absence, for as well as Marcus being in Kent with his father, Sir Wolford and Sir Henry Clavell were both in Bristol on business to do with their joint venture and were not expected home for several days. The servants might well doubt her story that she'd taken it into her head to go for an early morning ride without a groom in attendance, but they would hold their tongues.

She rode round to the back of the house, dismounted, and led Simon's horse into the stable yard where, as arranged, the porter was waiting. She had expected some muttered surly comment but he said nothing, only looked at her with an unpleasant gleam, almost of satisfaction, in his eye before he took what was obviously a strange mount away to be stabled.

Quietly she opened the back door into the kitchen and the servants' quarters confident that she would now be able to slip up to her room unobserved. But instead of the silence of a sleeping household there was noise, lights and movement, signs of an arrival, then Hannah appeared looking distressed, obviously having dressed in haste, as sleepy servants appeared down the backstairs, rubbing their eyes and yawning.

'Oh there you are, my lady, thank goodness,' Hannah greeted her with obvious relief. 'We couldn't understand why you weren't in your bed, we've been looking everywhere. You said nothing of spending the night from home. And the master not here either.'

'I've not been from home, only riding early,' Olivia replied. Then, filled with foreboding, she asked, 'Why was I being sought? What's happened?'

The housekeeper looked distraught. 'It's not for me to say, my lady. Sir Marcus is waiting for you in the living room.'

Olivia started to tremble and felt sick. Leaden footed she walked down the corridor to the large living room, now lit with branches of candles. Marcus was sitting at the big table looking towards the door and she could see at once that he was quite, quite sober. She tried to smile. 'What are you doing back here so soon, Marcus? I'd every intention of joining you later today.'

'Had you?' His eyes raked her from head to foot, taking in her stained and dirty clothing and tangled hair. 'I might also ask you the same. Where have you been, madam? And what are you doing up at this time of night or, to be more accurate, so early in the morning?'

'I was unable to sleep. I went for an early-morning ride.'

He gave her an unpleasant and disbelieving smile. 'I returned home some half hour ago, Olivia, but did not find you in our bed which was cold and had obviously not been slept in. No one could tell me where you were and while they might well all be lying, they assured me you'd said nothing of spending a night from home.'

She opened her mouth but was unable to speak.

'You see I'm here because Father died yesterday. Therefore I returned to fetch my loving and faithful wife back to Kent with me; once I've discussed various matters of importance with your father.'

She swallowed hard. 'I am very sorry that Lord Tuckett is dead and of course I will go back to Kent with you at once. But as for my father, he's now in Bristol with Sir Henry Clavell and not expected back until the end of the week.'

Marcus stood up. 'When it became obvious that my father was dying and nothing could save him, I sent a messenger to Sir Wolford as he had given me his direction in Bristol and he sent word back to me at once. He is now on his way home and likely to arrive at any time.' He walked over to her. 'And now, Olivia, perhaps you'll be so good as to tell me exactly where you've been and why.'

She cast around frantically for answers and was about to limp out a lame excuse when she heard the sound of a carriage rumbling to a halt outside and Hannah came running into the room to tell them that the master had returned from Bristol.

It was past dawn by the time Simon and John Bradedge

reached home. The driver, after helping carry Down into the same outbuilding which had once housed Eliza's body, was sent off with a warning to the effect that if he showed his face anywhere on the Bankside again he would be taken before a magistrate with the recommendation he be branded as a felon.

As they laid Down on the stone slab, he began to moan, asking where he was and what had happened.

Simon looked down at him. 'I'll tell you what happened, Down. You tried to kill me. Happily you didn't succeed. As to where you are, you're in my outhouse, the very same place to which we brought your victim.' Simon bent and peered closely at the wound on Down's scalp which was still bleeding sluggishly. 'I'll clean up your head and put a salve of amaranthus on it and I'll even go so far as to give you an old straw mattress to lie on. After which you'll stay tied up here until we take you back to Sir Wolford Barnes as a present. Don't fret – you'll survive to go to the gallows.'

He went back into his house hardly able to keep his eyes open. Anna, who had also spent a sleepless night, was sitting beside her husband with her child on her knee, thumb in mouth. She exclaimed with dismay when she saw the state of Simon, still covered in mud and with his clothes wet through.

'I've survived worse than this, Anna,' he said as he struggled out of his sodden boots. 'Now I want as much hot water for the tub as you can boil up. I smell like a midden and I need to give my side a soak where that bastard kicked me.' He turned to John. 'You should get some sleep if you can. When I've seen to Down's wound,

I intend going to bed myself for a couple of hours. We all need some rest before we pay a visit to Bishopsgate.'

Sir Wolford's arrival had proved fortuitous for it saved Olivia from having to answer Marcus. She immediately went out to greet her father and offer him breakfast. Given the unready state of the rest of the household, coupled with the fact that he was an unobservant man at the best of times, Sir Wolford made no comment on her bedraggled appearance. He called first for food and ale and then, after breakfasting with his son-in-law and now-silent daughter, he went to his desk and immediately sent for his secretary.

The servant bidden to fetch Francis Down returned within a few minutes saying he had been unable to find him. Sir Wolford then bawled for Hannah, telling her to go up to the attics and drag the lazy rascal out of bed at once, demanding to know if it was his custom to rise at noon when his master was from home. But Hannah too came back with the same tale. She had been unable to find him and, 'What's more, sir, his bed doesn't seem to have been slept in,' information which seemed to be of particular interest to Sir Marcus.

By this time a group of servants had assembled outside the door of the room, all eager to tell Sir Wolford that no one seemed to have seen Master Down since the previous day. Throughout all the frantic activity Sir Marcus said nothing, not even to Sir Wolford, but looked long and hard at his wife as if an idea was slowly beginning to form in his mind.

Sir Wolford turned to Olivia. 'You've been here all the time. Have you any idea where he is?'

She shook her head, avoiding her husband's eye. 'I've seen nothing of him since yesterday morning.' She was desperately tired but fearful of going to her room in case her husband followed her there and insisted on proper answers to his questions, answers she was unable to give. Finally, having shouted to all and sundry that as soon as Down showed his face he was to present himself before Sir Wolford at once, the merchant clapped Marcus on the shoulder and told him he was sorry to have been held up by so trivial a matter when there was much to discuss regarding his father's death which must be a sad loss to him.

Marcus did not appear unduly upset. 'It was expected and Father had put his affairs in order, or as much in order as they're ever likely to be. I'll have more freedom now, of course, but there's little I can to do to improve matters financially, for the estate is entailed and, mortgages or no mortgages, must be passed on in its entirety to my heir. If I ever have one, that is. Father died a disappointed man that it was not even in prospect.' He glanced sulkily at Olivia. 'I had expected your daughter to breed by now.'

'I'm not a brood mare to be taken to the stallion,' Olivia countered with some of her usual spirit. 'Your father could hardly have expected a guarantee.'

Sir Wolford looked from one to the other in some surprise. 'Well, there's nothing that can be done to change the present situation and now is hardly the time to discuss it.' He turned again to Marcus. 'When is your father to be buried?'

'Four days from now. The extra day is to allow for word to be sent to my two uncles and other members of the family to enable them to attend. I trust you'll also be able to do so, sir?'

Sir Wolford assured him that he would and that he would immediately despatch a messenger to his wife in Stratford St Anne asking her to leave at once for London to accompany him. Sir Marcus thanked him, then turned to other matters. The prospect of becoming head of the family appeared at least to have given him some backbone. 'Now, if you'd be so kind, I'd like you to look at the terms of my father's Will and some relevant papers. Then, after we've dined this noon, I intend leaving at once for Kent taking Olivia with me. There is much to do and as the new lady of the house it is her duty to see everything is fitting for the burial and that rooms are prepared for the family mourners.'

He spread the documents out on the table in front of Sir Wolford for him to read. 'Hell and damnation,' swore Sir Wolford, 'why in the Devil's name has Down taken it into his head to go off just when I need him?'

Grateful for the opportunity their discussion provided, Olivia slipped away to her bedroom and locked the door. She struggled out of her clothes, fell on the bed and in spite of her fears, sleep overtook her as she tried to invent an excuse for her absence from home overnight that her husband could not disprove even if he did not believe it.

★   ★   ★

In the middle of the morning Anna tapped on Simon's bedroom door to tell him that the religious gentleman was downstairs waiting to see him. Simon sat up and blinked at the light. His head still ached and in spite of having drunk pints of water and ale his mouth remained dry. Gingerly he inspected the rest of the damage. His wrists and the lower parts of his arms were sore from the ropes and he had a nasty bruise where Down had kicked him in the ribs. Calling to Anna that he'd be down shortly, he dressed as quickly as he could, wincing as he did so, then went downstairs where he found James Field sitting in the kitchen with John Bradedge who had obviously been giving him a colourful account of the night's events.

Field shook Simon warmly by the hand. 'Thank God you have come through safely,' he said. 'When I heard nothing this morning I did as you asked and read your letter, then, having waited a little while longer, I felt duty bound to come here to see if I could discover what had happened to you. I must tell you that I feared for your life.'

'That I'm still around to tell the tale is entirely due to John here,' returned Simon with a smile. 'Fearing that something like this might happen, he disobeyed my orders and followed me out to Brentford. It's clear I've much to learn before I allow myself to become involved in any further affairs of this nature. Should I ever wish to do so,' he added, 'which I doubt.'

'You were obviously destined to be the doctor's guardian angel on this occasion, Master Bradedge,' said Field, 'so enabling us to trap a nest of vipers.' He then enquired as to the whereabouts of Francis Down.

'Tied up in my outhouse with a sore head,' Simon told him. 'I plan to deliver him to his master as soon as I've breakfasted and was hoping you might care to join me.'

Field smiled with satisfaction. 'I suppose it's not very Christian of me but I have to say I shall be only too delighted.'

Around the middle of the morning, Sir Wolford's porter was summonsed to the gate by a prolonged ringing of the bell. Standing outside was a well-dressed clerical gentleman accompanied by a burly man with a scar on his face. They had obviously descended from a carriage which was waiting in the street behind them. On being informed that Dr James Field, rector of Stratford St Anne, wished to see Sir Wolford Barnes on urgent business, the porter opened the gate a few inches then made his usual surly response telling them they were to wait where they were while he went to find out whether Sir Wolford – who had only just returned from journeying all night and was much exercised with grave affairs – was prepared to see them.

He then made to close the gate but John, advised of this procedure, immediately put his shoulder to it and, forcing himself through the gap, caught held of the man, twisted one of his arms behind his back with one hand while pricking him in the back with a dagger held in the other. 'You will,' he hissed to the shocked porter, 'be silent and do as you're told or I'll stick this right through you. Believe me. I never make idle threats.'

Field meanwhile had gone back to the carriage and helped Simon haul out the recalcitrant Francis Down, still plastered in mud, his hands tied behind him and with a scarf over his mouth. Once they were all inside the gate Simon demanded the porter's key which he took and locked the gate from the inside. The strange party then made its way to the front door which was standing ajar. As they reached it, John dragged the porter round a corner, tied his hands, gagged his mouth and dumped him under a convenient bush. He then rejoined the others.

The house was quiet, the servants about their work and there was no one to hinder them as they walked swiftly up the hall towards the room into which Simon had been shown on his first visit and where it was obvious they would find Sir Wolford for they could hear his voice booming through the door.

Field pushed it open and went in first. Sir Wolford was sitting beside his son-in-law at a large table on which a number of documents were spread out. He looked at his uninvited guest in astonishment.

'Field? God's blood, what are you doing here? Who let you in? No word was sent that I was to expect you.' He made a gesture of dismissal. 'Well, whatever the purpose of your visit might be, I can't see you now. I've urgent matters to attend to. You must call some other time and give me notice of your intention – that is if your flock in Stratford St Anne can spare you.'

Field smiled, pulling out a chair and sitting down as if he had been invited to do so. 'I apologise for my un-orthodox arrival, Sir Wolford, but I can assure you that however urgent your business is it can't be as pressing as mine. Come in, Dr Forman,' he called out over his shoulder and Simon appeared, followed by John Bradedge, pushing Francis Down along in front of him. John then closed the door and leant against it, his drawn sword in his right hand.

Sir Wolford rose to his feet apoplectic with rage. 'What the Devil's the meaning of this, Forman? How dare you set foot in my house! Have you still not learned your lesson? This time it won't be your licence you'll lose but your liberty. You'll go to gaol and when I've finished, they'll throw away the key.' It was then he noticed the prisoner. 'Down? Why are you in that state? Have these brigands set on you? Release him at once!' he ordered.

Nothing happened. He rounded on Sir Marcus. 'Don't just sit there like a stock, go and tell the porter to fetch the constable here at once and bring some strong men with him.'

Marcus looked round for his sword which he had taken off and left suspended on its hanger over the back of the chair. 'Ah-ah,' said Simon. 'I shouldn't try and use that pretty toy if I were you. Both I and my servant are well armed as you can see and he is holding the door. As to going to gaol, there are certainly those now among us who will shortly be spending time there, preparatory to going to Tyburn. Do sit down, Sir Wolford, you look overheated.' The merchant sat as if his legs had given way under him. 'I think,' Simon continued, 'that your daughter should be present at the discussion we are about to have for it involves her closely.'

Marcus made a stealthy movement at his side causing Simon to pause. 'Before either reaching for your dagger or calling for help, I must tell you that the information we are about to impart has also been laid this morning before a magistrate: information which should be of quite particular interest to you, Sir Marcus. I suggest you hear what it is before doing anything rash. Now, I will go and seek out a maid and ask her to fetch your daughter.'

He did so, returning to find Sir Wolford had regained sufficient strength to be demanding still the immediate release of Francis Down. Simon went so far as to remove the scarf from the secretary's mouth. 'This man has no one to blame but himself for the pass he finds himself in,' he said. 'And I suggest you leave any further questioning until your daughter is here.'

Olivia was woken from a restless sleep by a wide-eyed maid, breathless with excitement, who told her that a party of gentlemen were with her father and that she was to go down to them at once. Olivia struggled awake, then called for water to wash her face, dragged a comb through her hair and told the girl to hand her the nearest clean gown and help her put it on. There was no time to do any more. She wondered who the men were and why there was need for such haste, but felt grateful for any diversion in the circumstances. Surely, too, Francis Down must have returned by now and would be able to tell her how he had disposed of Simon Forman.

She opened the door of the room and stood aghast at the scene that confronted her. Her father was sitting in his usual chair, his face flushed an unhealthy red. Marcus sat beside him, his fingers gripping the edge of the table and a look on his face she had never seen before. Standing facing them was the man she had been assuming was dead, while his would-be assassin, covered in mud and with his head roughly bandaged, leant against the wall, shivering in his wet clothes. Dr James Field, the clergyman from Stratford St Anne, sat in a chair, his face grim. She came into the room and the door closed behind her of its own accord as John Bradedge took up his position again. The blood drained from her face. Simon offered her a chair which she accepted.

'Now,' said Sir Wolford, apparently speaking with some difficulty, 'perhaps you'd finally be so good as to explain yourselves.' He looked at John Bradedge leaning on the door. 'You can't keep us prisoners much longer. I will shout to the first servant who knocks on that door to muster all the help he can to break in and release us. I'll make sure that when you come to trial for what you have done the whole of London will know of it.'

Simon looked at him with a wry smile. 'I wonder. Well, put briefly, this man here,' he pulled Down upright again and shook him by the shoulder, 'murdered your daughter's maid, Eliza, and we have proof of this. He was also prepared to murder me but we will come to that later.

'As you of all people know, I wasn't satisfied as to the cause of the girl's death or the possible reasons given for it and was thus driven – you might say by those old-fashioned virtues truth and justice – to find out what really happened, as a result of which you did your best to deprive me of my livelihood. But by doing this you should have realised I'd nothing more to lose. Therefore I continued my investigations which, yesterday, took me out to the Three Pigeons in Brentford at the request of your daughter.'

Sir Wolford banged his fist on the table. 'You expect me to believe this foolery, Forman? It's not gaol you need, it's the madhouse.' He turned to Marcus. 'Have you ever heard anything so crazed?' But Sir Marcus did not respond as expected, looking at Olivia as if much had finally become clear.

'Your daughter said the same to me in a private room at the Three Pigeons last night,' continued Simon. 'At that time I had only the barest proof. Now I have enough to destroy you all.'

'And what have you to say to this, Down?' broke in Sir Wolford again. 'Come, man, you can surely defend yourself against these monstrous charges.'

It was obvious the man's mouth was so dry he could hardly speak. Simon dragged a jug of ale across the table from where it had been placed close to Sir Wolford, poured some into a cup and handed it to Down to drink. The secretary raised his head. 'Like you, Sir Wolford, I think this man is quite mad. What he's told you is a farrago of lies. He said the same to me when he assaulted me without warning.'

At this point Sir Marcus rose to his feet. 'Before we go any further, Sir Wolford, I too would like answers to some questions. Perhaps your daughter would be good enough to explain to me what she was doing in Brentford last night with this busy doctor. When I arrived from Kent she was not in the house and didn't return home until the small hours and gave no other explanation either for that or for the state she was in, other than that she was sleepless and had been riding early. And was this fellow here,' he looked at Down, 'gallivanting around the countryside with her?'

Olivia looked from one to the other. 'You can't possibly believe any of this, surely? This man,' she gestured to Forman, 'has pursued me since he first visited our house for reasons I couldn't understand until last night. Yesterday I did indeed ride out into the country as I felt the need of air and exercise and, yes, I took Master Down with me as protection. It seems Dr Forman must somehow have discovered my intention and followed me for when we stopped for refreshment before returning home, he suddenly burst into the room where I was sitting alone, telling me he had information he must impart with regard to Eliza's death.'

'And where was the faithful Master Down during all this?' enquired Sir Marcus. 'Sitting beside you taking notes?' When not sodden with drink it seemed he could be quite sharp.

'Master Down was eating with other servants as was proper,' Olivia retorted. 'I asked Dr Forman to come quickly to the point as it was getting late and I wished to return home. Whereupon he flung himself at me, dragged me to a couch and tried to rape me, telling me that he had long desired me and was determined to have his way. I fought him to the best of my ability but would have failed to remain unravished had not Master Down entered the room to find out when we were to return to London.'

'There you have it!' bawled Sir Wolford. 'You'll hang for this, Forman.'

'I am, of course, grateful that your virtue was preserved, Olivia,' Sir Marcus continued, 'but it hardly explains why Down is standing here with his hands bound and a broken head.'

Olivia paused for a moment too long then replied, 'We thought he had driven Dr Forman away but on our way back to London where the road is lonely he set on us, assisted by his servant there.' She pointed to John Bradedge.

Field, who had sat silent throughout the interchange, then intervened. 'Enough of this! I will explain more fully later, if necessary, how I became involved in this affair but suffice it to say that when Dr Forman was passing through Stratford St Anne . . .' (Sir Wolford made a noise of disbelief) '. . . through Stratford St Anne, we discussed the girl's death as he was present when she was buried. Afterwards, when he went to pay his respects to the family, the girl's mother told him that her daughter had brought home a hundred guineas in gold and that although she and her husband had questioned her closely she had refused to divulge its origin, except to say that it was not obtained by theft.'

'See,' said Sir Wolford looking up at his son-in-law, 'he's also one of this crazed conspiracy.'

Field ignored the interruption. 'Later Mistress Pargeter confided in me and also showed me the money. This, coupled with information I had requested from Dr Forman on the subject of drowning, gave me great cause for concern. A man in my position is all too well aware of human frailty and it occurred to me that so large a sum of money might well have been given to this girl to ensure she held her tongue on some matter which could have plunged her mistress of your household into a public scandal. I must also say I fully support the actions Dr Forman has taken. He has had no other choice.'

Simon thanked him. 'I had reached the same conclusion,' he said. 'Also, when Lady Tuckett came to consult me at my house – oh, I can assure you she did,' he added, as Sir Wolford made a sound of disbelief, 'I was struck by a fleeting physical resemblance between herself and her maid, although I did not make the true connection until she and I discussed the matter – at her invitation – in a private room at the Three Pigeons. There was no attempted rape and I imagine the ostlers will remember my being dragged insensible into a carriage by its driver and Down.'

'But why should my secretary have done as you allege?' demanded Sir Wolford.

'Because, so your daughter told me, she had to rid herself of her maid who, having been paid once for her silence, became greedy and came back for more. She asked Down to see to it for her. She informed me, with tears in her eyes, that she had never intended the girl's death but that he had wickedly overruled her.'

At this Francis Down lost all control. 'So that's your game, lady! I'm to be thrown to the wolves to save you! Did you also tell Forman how you begged and pleaded with me, first to get rid of the girl, then himself? How you hired a cutthroat to try and prevent his giving evidence at the Inquest? You are as guilty as if you were at my side throughout everything. And do you know why Eliza Pargeter had to be silenced?' he said directly to Sir Marcus.

'No,' said Olivia getting to her feet, 'no!' She looked wildly round at the others. 'Whatever he says, don't believe him!'

Down looked at Sir Marcus with contempt. 'Because she paid the girl to change places with her on her wedding night because she knew her husband would realise she was not a virgin. You were duped, Sir Marcus, drugged with wine laced with poppy syrup. You lay with the maid that night, not the mistress.'

Sir Marcus went over to Down, grabbed him by the front of his doublet and shook him. 'I've long had my suspicions of you and your sly ways. Why were you prepared to do all this? And what other services have you performed for my wife?'

'How can you let him stand there and insult me?' cried Olivia. 'A mere hired man. Look at him. I don't know what he's been doing or where he's been or why he's accusing me of these terrible things.' She made a move to go to her father but Marcus, releasing Down, caught hold of her instead.

'What really passed at Brentford last night, Olivia? Are you and Forman lovers?'

At this Down burst into loud laughter. 'He's not her lover! I, the mere "hired man" bedded your wife long before she was betrothed to you – and after. Nor was I the first. The lady has a taste for it. And there's something

230

else you should know.' He laughed again. 'You knew the maid was with child? It was yours!'

Sir Marcus made a lunge for Down's throat and would have squeezed the life out of him had Simon and Field between them not prevented it. 'Leave him!' ordered the clergyman as Down gasped for breath. 'He will pay his account in this world and the next. Leave it to God and the Law.'

A strangled sound came from Sir Wolford who slumped back in his chair, breathing heavily, but Sir Marcus ignored him, turning again to Olivia. 'Is this true? Tell me, slut, is this true? Don't worry,' he said as she backed away from him, 'I'll not waste good steel on you.'

Olivia lifted her head. 'I was sold to you, Marcus, by my father there like any other commodity he bought and sold. I had little say in the matter. That too was a bargain: his wealth for your title. Yes, I've had lovers. A player who I truly loved. And Francis Down because I was bored and wanted pleasure and he was available.'

Sir Marcus gazed on her in horror. 'You killed my child,' he said. 'Not only the girl but my child as well. You're worse than a Bankside whore.'

'And of what worth are you?' she replied. 'A drunken sot who passes his days in gaming houses and brothels. I've lived in dread of your giving me the pox each time you lay with me.'

It was as if they had forgotten their audience. Marcus took Olivia by the hand and pulled her round the table to her father. 'Here, take her back. I want no soiled goods. It's as well you aren't with child after all,' he told her, 'for how would I know if it was mine?'

Sir Wolford tried to get to his feet, his breath rasping in his throat, his face now purple. He tried to speak but only noise came from his mouth. Then he fell heavily on to the table in front of him. Simon immediately went over to him and pulled him back into his chair. 'Call your servants,' he said to Olivia and her husband, 'he must be got to bed. I will do what I can for him but he's mortally sick.'

'It's no longer any concern of mine,' returned Sir Marcus. 'I shall leave at once for Kent. Once my father is buried, Olivia, I will have this marriage annulled. I never want to see or hear from you ever again.'

'But what will become of me?' she asked desperately.

'Why should I care? Go peddle your wares where you can. That is if you don't find yourself standing side by side on the scaffold with your lover.' He walked to the door which John Bradedge opened for him and then out of the house.

Simon called for the servants, some of whom appeared so quickly that they must have been hovering close by, aware that something was badly amiss. Hannah entered the room first and cried out with alarm at the sight of her master lying in his chair unable to move hand or foot. 'Get two of your fellows to fetch a hurdle from the yard,' Simon told her, 'so that we can lay him on it and carry him to his chamber.'

As he went to do so he told John to take Down outside and find somewhere secure to put him until the constable arrived. 'You'd better also release the porter though I don't envy you the task. I can only hope my horse is here somewhere too as I'm in no position to afford another,' added Simon with a sigh. The hurdle was brought and Sir Wolford placed on it and he was carried up the stairs but with some difficulty for he was a heavy man and a dead weight. Simon and Olivia brought up the rear of the procession.

'You realise the authorities will have to be fully informed of all this?' he said. 'I spoke truly when I said we'd already laid information against Down and he will certainly stand trial. Whether or not he chooses also to involve you is another matter. But now I must see what I can do for your father.'

'Will he live?' she asked.

'That's in the hands of the Almighty, but I doubt it.' He called down to James Field who was standing at the foot of the stairs. 'I think you should also attend him, sir, for he will have need of a man of God if he intends making his peace with this world.'

Olivia smiled wryly at the clergyman. 'It would seem you are in luck, parson. If my father dies there'll be no heir now to keep you from your estate.' As they reached the door of her father's bedchamber she stopped and put her hand on Simon's arm. 'You appear to have won most of the moves in this game, Dr Forman,' she said, 'but don't assume you've won them all.'

Epilogue

'Dead?' roared Simon. 'You say he's *dead*? How can he possibly be dead?'

John Bradedge shrugged. 'That's what the turnkey at the gaol told me. He said Down was taken with terrible stomach cramps in the night and died before morning. And he due to come to trial tomorrow.'

June had passed into July, the weather still fitful but with some days of sunshine like this one. After writing up his notes, Simon had been out in his herb garden. Designing it and then planting out the chosen herbs was the only pleasure he had retained from his rural origins, of the Quidhampton farm labourer's son who had so thankfully escaped. He found it relaxing and soothing. It also required skill, not only of a horticultural nature but because the efficacy of many herbs depended on their being planted at the right phase of the moon or when their particular planet was in the ascendant. The scent of the herbs filled the air.

He still felt in limbo. Dr Field had left promising he would do everything in his power to see the Royal College of Physicians gave Simon back his licence and he had been as good as his word, not only writing to them but returning to London to see the president in person. They were obviously in no hurry to take a decision but in the meantime Simon had been warily visiting old patients in the City and Blackfriars, so far without any trouble.

Field's task had been made easier because, as Simon had expected, Sir Wolford died of his apoplexy after having lingered on unconscious for a week. The funeral had been a muted occasion which hadn't gone unremarked. Of Olivia Tuckett he had heard nothing and had assumed Francis Down must have undergone a change of heart and said nothing of her involvement or, that if he had done so, had been disbelieved. Sir Wolford might be dead and the Tucketts estranged but neither they nor Sir Wolford's City colleagues would want an open scandal. Down had provided them with a convenient scapegoat and Simon was in no doubt that every effort had been made to see it stayed that way.

But now, if John Bradedge's information was correct there would be no trial and Down had cheated the gallows after all. Simon went back into the house and washed the soil off his hands. So, now nothing would ever come out and Sir Thomas Monkton could rest easy with his verdict. He reached for his doublet and hat. 'I'll be back before noon,' he told the Bradedges. 'I'm away to Sir Wolford's house, then to Newgate.'

Simon walked through the busy Bankside to London Bridge. Life had gone on as usual while he had been wrestling with the problem of Eliza's death. The whole episode now seemed unreal, like something viewed at a playhouse. The notion of the playhouse made him glance back towards the Rose Theatre where a flag was flying to show there would be a performance that afternoon.

As he crossed the bridge he thought of Olivia and what she'd said to him after the collapse of her father. Brave words or did she really have something still up her sleeve? His mind strayed to that evening at the Three Pigeons and what might well have happened had he not been drugged. Certainly not rape; he was as sure as he could be that her attraction towards him had been quite genuine even if she had been quite prepared to use it for her own purposes. A night with Olivia would surely have been a night to remember. However he now had hopes elsewhere for twice in recent days he had seen the enticing Avisa Allen on her way to visit her uncle, and on the latter occasion she had blushed prettily and told him she was planning to visit him to discuss a small matter regarding her health. He was looking forward to that.

Even though it was only a few weeks since Sir Wolford's death his house had an air of slight neglect. There was no sign of the porter and when Simon rang the bell it was answered by Hannah. He asked if he could speak to Olivia.

Lady Tuckett, Hannah told him, had gone away but she'd go and ask Lady Barnes if she would see him. 'Poor lady, she's much pulled down by all this trouble,' she said with a sigh, 'and she was never robust at the best of times.'

She took him into the house and asked him to wait in the hall while she asked the mistress if she felt strong enough for visitors. She returned within a few minutes and showed Simon into a small sitting room. Lady Barnes, a faded replica of her portrait, lay on a small couch, her knees covered with a rug. She waved a hand towards a chair.

'I trust this won't take long, Dr Forman. You can see I am weak and far from well.'

Simon assured her that he would not take much of her time, said untruthfully that he was sorry to hear of the death of her husband and informed her that he was hoping to have spoken to her daughter. It was clear Lady Barnes knew very little of what had passed or his part in it, only the dire results: that she had been forced to remove from the Essex estate, where she was happy, to the town where she was not, and that Marcus, now Lord Tuckett, was refusing any longer to live with Olivia as his wife.

'What will come of it all I don't know nor why we have been so singled out for misfortune,' she complained. As for Olivia, 'My daughter left for Paris last night. My late husband has a business associate there and she has gone to visit his family and expects to be away several months.' Until after the trial of Francis Down, thought Simon wryly. Except that she need not have worried since the man was now dead. He wondered if a possible escape to France was what she'd had in mind when she'd said the game was not yet over. There was obviously nothing to be gained by questioning Lady Barnes any further and he took his leave and made his way towards Newgate.

So Lady Barnes was alone in that great house. He wondered if she would remain in it now without her husband or the social life that would have come from

Olivia and Marcus using it when they were in town for themselves and their prospective children. But what had been painful for Lady Barnes had proved enormously pleasurable to James Field.

He was thoroughly enjoying coming into his inheritance. Simon had asked him if he would still act as rector to the parish and he had said he was planning to continue for the time being, though he would be looking out for a suitable curate to see to its day-to-day running. He was, he said, surprised to find he had become fond of his flock.

As to the Pargeters, he had told them as much of the story as he'd felt they should know. 'At least,' he wrote to Simon, 'they have the satisfaction of knowing the main culprit will come to trial and I've also assured them that their tenancy and employment on the estate are secure. As to the hundred guineas, as they'd no knowledge of how it was got, I see no reason why they shouldn't keep it.' He had ended his letter assuring Simon that he would be very welcome to visit himself and his family at any time in the future.

Simon was now in the shadow of Newgate. Would Francis Down, when all that lay before him was the prospect of the hangman's rope, have implicated Olivia in a final gesture of revenge? Well, that was now academic. He went up to the great door, peered through the grille, and asked the turnkey on duty if he might see the Head Gaoler. His request was met with a blank stare until money changed hands after which the door was opened and the man shuffled ahead of him down a dank corridor. The stench of the overcrowded cells wafted up from below causing Simon to bury his face in his handkerchief.

The Head Gaoler was to be found in his own small room or office which was little cleaner than the passageway outside. He was sitting at a battered table poring over a small pile of documents, an open bottle of brandy beside him. He knew Simon by sight for, on occasion, he had sent for him to see to the needs of a sick prisoner who had enough money to pay for a physician. Many doctors would not even set foot in the prison.

He gestured towards the papers. 'Tyburn fodder,' he said. 'Tomorrow's hangings. So, Doctor, what do you want?'

'It's to do with one of your inmates who was certainly bound for that same place. He was to have come to trial tomorrow but I hear he's cheated you at the last.'

The Head Gaoler frowned. 'Who's that?'

'A man called Francis Down. He was once secretary to the late Sir Wolford Barnes, the merchant venturer. I'm told he's dead.'

'And what interest is it of yours?'

Simon explained that he had taken a hand in the man being brought to justice. 'Also because his death comes as a surprise for when I last saw him he was in good health, except for a slash on the scalp. And I've not heard you are much afflicted either with gaol fever or the bloody flux at present.'

The man agreed they were not and that Down had been fortunate in having sufficient funds for him to have a room of his own – a real luxury as otherwise he'd have been in one of the big communal cells – and so was less likely to have come into contact with infection. He'd even been able to hire a mattress to sleep on, buy candles to see by and send out for food. 'So they can't say he died because of what he ate in here,' he concluded.

'Did he have any visitors?'

'Why?' returned the gaoler, looking suddenly shifty.

'Well, did he?' demanded Simon.

The man scratched his groin. 'Pest on these fleas,' he grumbled. 'Some woman came yesterday,' he admitted finally. 'Gave me a guinea to talk with the prisoner. Couldn't see any harm in it.'

'What did she look like?'

'Couldn't really tell. She'd a great cloak on with a hood hiding most of her face. Well spoken, though. I'd say gentry. I assumed she must be his doxy. Many such like a bit of the rough stuff when it comes to a tumble. But you probably know that in your trade.'

'Did she bring anything with her?' Simon persisted.

'She brought him food and drink in a basket. Showed me a pie and some oranges and two bottles of wine. There was nothing else there, I looked.'

Simon should have known. It had to be, of course. So Olivia had played her final card after all. He wondered what had passed between the two at that last meeting when she had brought Down his dainty supper, where she had managed to obtain the poison she must have put in the wine and what it was she had used. Monkshood? Not quick enough. Belladonna? The symptoms were wrong. Possibly one of the mineral poisons. Now he would never know.

'Is that all?' grunted the Head Gaoler.

Simon said that it was and that he would not keep him from his task any longer. The man shrugged. 'Don't you want to know who she was?' he asked.

Simon looked at him in amazement. Surely Olivia hadn't been brazen enough to give her real name. The Head Gaoler reached over to a shelf and lifted down a large, tattered book. He opened it and worked his way through to the previous day's lists, down which he ran a grimy finger. Then he turned it round towards Simon so he could see the signature.

Written in a clear, bold hand was the name 'Eliza Pargeter'.

Author's Note

THE REAL DOCTOR SIMON FORMAN

Almost the only knowledge we had of him for a long time was the note in the *National Dictionary of Biography*, written by Sir Sydney Lee in the late 1870s, which is full of inaccuracies and described him as a charlatan and a quack, a view presumably he had taken after reading of the clashes Simon Forman had over a period of years with the Royal College of Physicians. Later research, for much of which we are indebted to Dr A. L. Rowse, shows he was very far from that and indeed that he had many new ideas gleaned from the Continent which were in advance of those prevailing in the England of his day. As an example, he did not believe in wholesale blood-letting, a common practice then and for centuries afterwards, as he considered it merely weakened the patient. Nor did the fact that he practised astrology, cast horoscopes and also used them for diagnoses make him a quack; most doctors did so then, including one of the earliest respected presidents of the Royal College of Physicians.

Simon Forman was born in Quidhampton, Wiltshire, probably in 1558, the youngest of five children. His father, who worked on the land, died when he was very young, leaving the family far from well off. After going to the village Dame school, he achieved a place at the local grammar school where he was considered a bright scholar. He was fascinated by the New Science and wanted to study medicine, and his teachers were eager that he should go to Oxford University, but, hardly surprising in her circumstances, his mother was unsympathetic towards his ambitions. The best he could manage was, when possible, to act as servant to a local parson's son who was a student at Oxford and attend some lectures, but he was not allowed to become a student himself as he had no funds and had not been offered a scholarship.

After a year he returned to Wiltshire to find work locally. He soon upset the local landowner, Giles Estcourt, as a result of which he spent nearly a year in prison. There is then a great blank after which we find him working as a medical practitioner in Salisbury (during which time he fathered an illegitimate child) before moving on to London where he set up as a qualified physician formally recognised by the University of Cambridge. He may or may not have studied in Italy (or elsewhere on the Continent) but he certainly studied somewhere and I decided on Italy for the purposes of this story.

When he first set up in practice in London he was endlessly hauled up before the College of Physicians who refused to recognise him as a doctor, even when his status was confirmed by Cambridge. They disliked his attitude, considered him an upstart who had risen from the ranks of the poor, and were the most likely source for the rumour that he was a necromancer who practised the Black Arts.

Dr Rowse dates his setting up in London as around 1593–94, and it has been suggested that on one occasion Queen Elizabeth's great Spymaster, Sir Francis Walsingham, intervened on his behalf to prevent his being sent to prison by the Royal College of Physicians. If this is indeed the case, then he must have been practising in London as early as 1590 for Walsingham died in the spring of that year.

Certainly by the early 1590s Simon Forman was living in a good house near to the Bankside (outside the jurisdiction of the City of London) with a garden in which he grew herbs and flowers for his medicines. He treated patients both at his own home and by visiting them, and he almost uniquely crossed the entire social spectrum from the publicans, actors, writers and whores of the Bankside, through the City merchants to the aristocracy and the Court. He enjoyed the theatre, leaving us the first accounts of seeing Shakespeare's plays, and Shakespeare's Bankside landlady was one of his patients as was the wife of Richard Burbage. He had a tremendous weakness for women and was candid about sex. He had a code word (*halek*) for those ladies who paid him in kind rather than in cash. He also had a brief, if stormy, affair with the strongest contender for the role of Shakespeare's Dark Lady, Emilia Lanier, née Bassano.

The long-term love of his life was, however, Avisa Allen who was married to a merchant older than she was and who also 'distilled', that is made medicines from herbs. Since he outlived her and divorce was out of the question there was no question of marriage. She became his mistress and their relationship continued until she died. Many years later he married Jane Baker, the daughter of a Kentish knight. He was an expert on poisons and death, and would have been a witness in the trial of Lady Howard for the murder of Sir Thomas Overbury, but he died suddenly just before the trial, from what might well have been appendicitis.

Simon Forman, like many doctors of his age including Shakespeare's son-in-law, John Hall, kept a meticulous Casebook of his patients and their maladies, and also of the horoscopes he cast. Forman also wrote books both on medicine and astrology. While my portrayal of Simon Forman owes much to poetic licence it is clear that the original was lively, clever and energetic and never ceased to have an enquiring mind.

The history of his servants, John and Anna Bradedge, is much as given in Chapter 2, although they entered his life somewhat later than in this story. However Sir Wolford Barnes, his daughter Olivia, Sir Marcus Tuckett and Dr James Field are purely imaginary.

THE BED-SWITCH PLOT

Servants who change places with their masters or mistresses date right back to the Roman dramatist, Plautus, and that plot, along with those where twins are mistaken for each other, was very popular with Elizabethan and Jacobean audiences.

Shakespeare made good use of both. Mistaken twins feature in the comedies *Comedy of Errors* and *Twelfth Night*. In *The Taming of the Shrew* Lucentio changes places with his servant, Tranio, so that he can court Kate's sister Bianca.

The 'bed-switch plot', where one woman is substituted for another in a man's bed was a mark of more serious drama. Shakespeare used it twice. In *All's Well That Ends Well* the unpleasant Bertram refuses to sleep with his unwanted wife, Helena, telling her he will only accept her as his wife if she becomes pregnant by him. In order to accomplish this impossible task she changes places with Diana, the woman he has fallen in love with. In *Measure for Measure*, after the repressive ruler, Angelo, has told the heroine, Isabella, that he will save her brother from execution only if she goes to bed with him, Isabella persuades Angelo's jilted fiancée, Mariana, to take her place.

The most striking example, however, which provided some of the inspiration for this story, is that of *The Changeling* by Thomas Middleton and William Rowley, one of the greatest of all the Jacobean tragedies. In it the amoral Beatrice Joanna persuades the family steward, who is in love with her, to murder her fiancé so she can wed another man. But his price is her virginity. Learning that her husband-to-be is devising methods of finding out whether or not she is a virgin, she persuades her maid to change places with her on her wedding night with tragic consequences. But in *The Changeling* the maid, though crucial to the plot, is a minor character, a mere innocent victim. *Death of a Lady's Maid*, however, is set well before the dates of these plays, so Olivia couldn't have got her idea from them.